"SUSAN CHACE HAS CONSTRUCTED A QUIVERING SLIVER OF MODERN URBAN ANGUISH."—*Los Angeles Times*

"Chace delicately combines memory and time present to sculpt her portrait of Cecilia, a woman almost in control. She uses language sparingly, creating surreal images that continue to haunt."—*The Detroit News*

"Sinewy . . . Her perfectly pitched, well-placed prose makes *Intimacy* a welcome fiction debut from an ex-journalist who never misses a beat."—*Vanity Fair*

"An affecting, insightful novel."—*People*

"The story takes off, backwards, forwards, through madness and sanity, childhood and adulthood . . . Chace's exploration of one woman's perceptions focuses a maelstrom of light on contemporary life."—*Booklist*

"In this beautifully controlled narrative, Chace reveals a probing intelligence and a compassionate heart."
—*Publishers Weekly*

"A woman's journey to self-understanding . . . Stylish . . . sharp and stripped down, with a nervous edge . . . Ms. Chace writes about childhood with a remarkable veracity and poignancy."—*The New York Times Book Review*

SUSAN CHACE is a former reporter with *Forbes* and *The Wall Street Journal*. *Intimacy* is her first novel.

INTIMACY

A NOVEL BY

SUSAN CHACE

A PLUME BOOK

NEW AMERICAN LIBRARY

A DIVISION OF PENGUIN BOOKS USA INC., NEW YORK

PUBLISHED IN CANADA BY
PENGUIN BOOKS CANADA LIMITED, MARKHAM, ONTARIO

Intimacy is a work of fiction. Any resemblance its characters
may have to persons living or dead is purely coincidental.

NAL BOOKS ARE AVAILABLE AT QUANTITY DISCOUNTS WHEN USED TO
PROMOTE PRODUCTS OR SERVICES. FOR INFORMATION PLEASE WRITE
TO PREMIUM MARKETING DIVISION, NEW AMERICAN LIBRARY,
1633 BROADWAY, NEW YORK, NEW YORK 10019.

Grateful acknowledgment is made to Farrar, Straus & Giroux, Inc.,
for permission to reprint from "Epilogue" from
Day by Day by Robert Lowell. Reprinted by permission of
Farrar, Staus & Giroux, Inc.

Portions of this work have appeared in
The Northwest Review and *The Paris Review.*

This is an authorized reprint of a hardcover edition
published by Random House, Inc.

PLUME TRADEMARK REG. U.S. PAT. OFF. AND FOREIGN COUNTRIES
REGISTERED TRADEMARK—MARCA REGISTRADA
HECHO EN BRATTLEBORO, VT., U.S.A.

SIGNET, SIGNET CLASSIC, MENTOR, ONYX, PLUME, MERIDIAN
and NAL BOOKS are published in the United States by
New American Library, a division of Penguin Books USA Inc.,
1633 Broadway, New York, New York 10019,
in Canada by Penguin Books Canada Limited,
2801 John Street, Markham, Ontario L3R 1B4

LIBRARY OF CONGRESS CATALOGING-IN-PUBLICATION DATA
Chace, Susan, 1942–
    Intimacy : a novel / by Susan Chace.
        p.   cm.
    ISBN 0-452-26375-1
    I. Title.
PS3553.H1815   1990
813'54.—dc   89-13377
                              CIP

Original hardcover design by Debbie Glasserman

First Plume Printing, February, 1990

    1 2 3 4 5 6 7 8 9

PRINTED IN THE UNITED STATES OF AMERICA

For Michael

τὸ μὴ δῦνόν ποτε πῶς ἄν τις λάθοι
–Heraclitus

How can you hide from what never goes away?

ACKNOWLEDGMENTS

◻

Thank you, James Chace and Zoe Chace. Thank you, David Rosenthal, Annik LaFarge and the staff at Random House. Thank you to my agent, Joe Spieler, and to Susan Lee, Lilla Lyon and Marcelle and Donald, and to Herman Roiphe and to J. J. Sempé.

INTIMACY

STICKUP

It's been two days since the mugging.

The oval face of the mugger rises higher and bobs in what looks like moonlight. Only it's raining.

The knife at my throat curves ever so slightly. It is shinier than it could really have been. The voice, more gentle: "Excuse me. Don't scream. Just give me your pocketbook." Only the fingers stay true, the touch of a jazz player, shaky, but secure on his turf. In an instant, he has slipped the straps off my shoulder. My handbag hangs from his wrist.

I feel deep, dead-end shame. The way it is when a lover lies to you, and you both know it's a lie.

It's the same scene in my head running over and over: I keep passing in front of the red fire hydrant under the super's window. My paper bag of groceries is soggy, except where I hold it with both arms around it. It smells good. When I get back inside, I'm going to tell my family how to behave if and when I ever cook them dinner again. After that display tonight, they are lucky I decided only to go around the block . . .

"Excuse me. Don't scream."

In my mind, I run like the wind and stay above interference.

In real life, I am flat-footed, and I follow instructions. "Turn around and walk. Don't look back."

Perhaps some history. I'm a thirty-seven-year-old journalist. Twice married. Three grown stepchildren. One new daughter, Addy, a tough kid, not at all the brooding beauty her brother Daniel is. Daniel's my son, now sixteen, originally lost in a custody case, lately returned to me with a message from his father, an eye doctor in Tucson: "Your son won't go to high school."

It was a victory, of course, to be handed Daniel back, ten years after the judge ruled he would live with his "stable" parent. But if the truth be told, it's been a time here this past month, complicated by the fact that the cause of turmoil is usually offstage. We don't see much of Daniel. He appears and disappears like the Cheshire cat. Even when he's in front of me, I get the feeling that I'm staring at what Gertrude Stein said about Oakland—there's no there there.

Case in point. The other night he showed up unexpectedly at the end of the bed. I usually know he's coming because his espadrilles squeak, but I must have been dreaming. Looking down from that halo of maroon-and-yellow hair, he said in his soft, spooky voice: "I need twenty dollars. Don't get up. Just point out your pocketbook." I did. "Thank you," he said and kissed me on the lips and was gone.

During the day, Daniel has a job as a messenger. He sleeps while we eat dinner. Then late at night he goes out dancing or into the living room and watches television—people like himself jumping out of windows or smashing through papier-mâché walls while holding on to guitars. It can be terrifying if you come upon it suddenly the way I do, around four in the morning. There's a kind of green glow in the living room at that hour. Daniel keeps the TV sound very low so as not to wake us, and that probably makes it stranger than it is. I mean all that screaming in pantomime. And once there was Daniel's silhouette against the far wall, dancing and screaming back to the TV. No sound.

Daniel thinks about noise. So do I. It's what I notice first. I still hear the moment my marriage to Daniel's father, Paul, ended. We were hanging a very large, square painting I had insisted on having. It's a picture of two high-back chairs, one with no legs, angled out toward the "horizon"—the point at which flat green ground meets a flat blue sky. The painting is called "Marriage," though I don't think Paul ever knew that. Anyway, I was holding one side of it, and my leg began to itch. I bent down to scratch and dropped my end of the painting. Paul screamed, a deafening curse I had never heard before. Only it wasn't a curse. It was my name.

I met Mark some years after that. He had had a full life already. So Daniel wasn't really news to him, or the custody case, or the institution for the mentally ill: "A long night ride on a stationary bicycle is what it sounds like," he said, sympathetically.

It was true we were worlds apart in that Mark liked to get up in the morning, and he didn't like white wine for breakfast. But, as it happened, the week before I met him, my shrink had introduced me to the notion of cooperation. I bit down hard, and I've been cooperating ever since. I even switched to business reporting to curb ungovernable urges. (Not even I get interested in a man if he talks about things like return on his equity.) Most of the time I hate cooperating, which seems to boil down to saying no to myself every time I want to say yes. There are often times I long for a little intrigue, some small debauchery, a good lie. Venial sin is what I'm into. I miss that flush on the cheeks, rising without warning—that old-time stirring, when I'd blush to see a lover seeing me, in a place where nothing could take place. (You may wonder how I know that's a venial sin. In high school we had a retreat priest who could actually measure desire.) Other times I long for the measure of the mythical tribe whose people had one of everything—one mate, one dog, one cat, one child. Each adult made love once in a lifetime, thinking about it a long time before, and remembering it for a long time afterwards.

It's interesting, these fused families: they work—I mean, the disintegration is minimal—but they don't count for much.

Case in point: There is a huge desk in our apartment that belonged to Mark during his first marriage. It's one of the things he mentions that have to be dealt with when he dies (any time soon, he warns us frequently). He can't figure out how to get it out of the building. He doesn't trust the movers, because the last time his desk was badly nicked. But he has to find a way to get it out when he's gone because it's "got to go to someone in the family." Family to Mark always means blood.

Here's the curve ball. Mark adores Daniel. You can see it in both their eyes when they drink beer and play each other music. Addy adores Daniel. She won't let anyone take off her T-shirt that says "Tucsonette" on it. "Me and Daniel," she says. She wants to be a boy when she grows up so she can wear earrings and makeup like Daniel does. Actually that's my makeup he's putting on before he goes out to those clubs.

I'm the only one with reservations. I'm the only one

who wants to beat up Daniel. For what? Staying up all night? Children don't take after strangers, after all. And look at him. He's a heartbreaker, my Daniel. Two packs of cigarettes gone in the night. Bloody bitten fingertips holding my hand when I shake him awake for work. "He's a smart kid, a little lost" is what Mark says.

"He's a vegetarian who hates vegetables. That's suicide" is what I say.

Food has become a big issue in this family since Daniel's arrived. Food and sleep. All of a sudden both are elusive. Addy hears me get up to look at Daniel, maybe. Anyway, she's started sleepwalking. Sometimes she wakes up Mark and asks him to fix her some bacon. It drives him crazy because he can't get back to sleep. If he doesn't sleep, he can't eat, and that's probably why I got mugged. I mean, if I hadn't blown up because nobody wanted my dinner, none of this would have happened.

It's Daniel who comes with me to the police station. Mark cooks eggs for Addy. Looking at the books in the precinct captain's office, I see the same moon-shadow face in every other picture, though I know in the calculating part of my mind that no two of the photographs look alike.

"Mom, some of these people are white and some are black," Daniel says, when I can't eliminate anyone.

"They are all have-nots, Daniel. I'm a have." (Am I

8

really such an idiot?) Daniel's coat stinks of cigarettes. I wish I still smoked.

The moonface swells in my sleep and explodes like a gum bubble when Daniel turns his key in the door. He went dancing after we left the police station. It must be close to daybreak by now. I'm not even sure it's Daniel coming home. Maybe it's the mugger. He would have keys too now. The mugger/Daniel is stumbling. A heavy plastic glass falls onto the bathroom tile floor.

I stand up in the bathroom light for a long time. Then I go to sleep with Addy. The bed creaks when I climb over her. I put her Sesame Street record back on, a song called "I Love Trash." It's a waltz. Addy cries a little and puts her thumb in her mouth. "Hello, my special-special," I say and work my arms around her. She is smaller than a grocery bag.

In the morning she rolls over on my head. "Excuse me," she says in high-tone two-year-old: "Did you sleep well?"

The day is bright and hot. Perfectly clear. A man telephones. His name is Howie Duggan, he says, and he has found my pocketbook in a trash can on Amsterdam and 74th Street, close to where we both live. He has taken it to where he works, in a locksmith shop on East 17th Street. "Thank you, Howie," I say, and dial the police, who want to meet "this Duggan guy."

Officer Ocotillo picks me up in front of the fire hydrant. We take the FDR Drive. "So now you are an official New Yorker," he says. Howie Duggan isn't around. He has left a cardboard container for me, the kind that holds beer and hot dogs at ball games. It says "Howei" on it. In this container, there is my checkbook, my date book, my reporter's notebook, my loose-leaf address book. I write a note to "Howei," thanking him and promising to send a reward.

At home, I lay paper towels on the dining-room table and spread out the pages of my address book. A watery blue blur of faces rises. The rain in the trash can has washed my sources and my contacts and my friends all together. Some of the names that haven't washed out I don't recognize. Who is Myrna Schultz?

Leo Crow's name is still there, even though he's dead. He was the building's old super, and he was a bully. He took his motorboat out on the lake one night when he was drunk. He never wore a life preserver. The boat turned over. Leo couldn't swim.

Names written in pencil are still easy to read: The IBM Product Center.

I find Robert Lowell's "Epilogue" stuck to a page in my checkbook. It's the poem that ends: "We are poor passing facts, warned by that to give each figure in the photograph its living name." I guess I like it so much because it's sort of a reporter's credo, or an ideal, maybe.

I mean, you can't ever reach it. "Pray for the grace of accuracy," Lowell advised.

When Jean Stafford, Lowell's first wife, got so sick she couldn't talk, she tried to get an interviewer to understand that she alone *knew* the story behind every word Lowell wrote. Does it make a difference if you know or not if you can't tell what you know?

I told that Arizona judge I knew Daniel, but through and through, the way a tree knows its leaves. I couldn't convince him. Daniel and I were still one body then, it seemed to me, even though he was already six years old.

But that's all water over the dam, so to speak. He's here now. With me. And every gesture is something out of a Magritte—detached, sudden—and solid with warning, possibly clairvoyant and possibly not.

Like when he fingered my shoulder before I stormed out into the rain: "You're not going to leave us, are you?" he said.

I guess they don't announce it these days, I mean they don't actually say the words "This is a stickup."

INDULGENCES

Long ago in cherry-blossom time, there was a man paddling a canoe down the Potomac River. It was a cold day, but the bright sun coming through the trees gave everything a dappled look, a kind of merriness. There was also, that particular day, a young woman on the shore. Flowers from the trees blew onto her bare head and shoulders. The man banked his canoe and went over, offering his jacket. And when the stars came out that evening, they could still be seen by the light of moon, scattering petals into the Potomac.

They eloped on her eighteenth birthday. Out of their union came a beautiful baby who never complained but instead grew daily in kindness and love. She died shortly before her seventh birthday.

Early on, I thought my dead sister and I were the same person. My mother held her picture to my face and searched and searched. "Me," I said confidently, "pretty me."

"No, not you. You are nothing like her."

"You have straight hair. That was your first mistake," said my aunt Fírinn. My mother's sister had an old-fashioned name. She said it meant "Truthful."

I was conceived on a bed of tears in Guadalajara. My mother and father went there after Elizabeth Anne's death to get away from their grief—from the cold tongue of February, from her white iron bed, from the cemetery where they heaped dirt on her coffin according to the Jewish custom. But every time they left the hotel, my mother's eyes picked out the gentlest little girl among the children playing by the banyan trees. My mother wept in Mexico. She collapsed on her bed in the hotel. My father tried to comfort her in the traditional way.

She cried all through the pregnancy.

"Your mother thought she had been punished for marrying a Jew. She called in a priest the night Elizabeth Anne died. He baptized her and gave her the last sacraments. She wasn't buried in Catholic ground, but it didn't matter because her soul was already in heaven," said my aunt Fírinn.

I have always known about death. It was above me in the icy pools of my mother's eyes, in the huge head bending down. It was a current in the air. When it hit my mother, she cried. When she cried, so did the baby, Martha, who came after me and slept in another crib. By then it was something dark we all breathed, like smoke. It was a stillness, a confinement.

But I have also always known about the life that comes after death. "You were baptized in your snowsuit. It was the coldest day in seventy years. The holy water in the font froze. You laughed and yipped all the way through it, but your mother caught pneumonia. If the Jews hadn't nailed Our Savior to a Cross, none of this would have happened," said my aunt Fírinn.

I have never enjoyed the winter. Spring is nice. In the early days, I made mud pies. I knew Elizabeth Anne had never made mud pies, never even wanted to try such a thing. I felt uneasy about how happy I was making mud pies and so I hid my operations in the back of the house behind the oak tree.

My mother sat in a big stuffed chair mending old socks. She pricked her finger often, though she used a thimble. She filled a jelly-jar glass with a clear liquid and spoke Ancient Knowledge: "On the day you are born, you have a path set for you. Time on earth is purgatory. This is my purgatory fire," she said to her darning pin. I played with the yarn. "This is my purgatory fire," I said to the yarn. I stared at the picture of my dead sister on the mantelpiece, and my mother took the picture down and put it in my hands. Elizabeth Anne wore a long white robe. She sat straight up in her hospital bed so she could touch cheeks with my mother. Her eyes were lit from the inside. I tried to look at her picture the way my father looked at it, with tears in his eyes but not dripping down. My father was away a lot. I guessed he was looking for Elizabeth Anne.

I knew what purgatory fire was. It was a smelly yellow place. I knew because I had been there.

One evening a dirty stench had spread all through the house. When we went outside, it was even worse. "A fire at the elastic factory," my mother said. The sky was yellow and gray and puffy. Martha was in the stroller and I was holding on to my mother. The smell pressed me close to her. We walked quite a ways and we stopped at a flat field. My mother left the sidewalk to pick up a large gray cardboard spool. It was charred at the upper and lower edges. It had a spindly little string of gray-white elastic wrapped around the middle. She put the spool in a bag in the stroller and looked down. Suddenly I saw that the field was covered with spools. I ran here and there, scooping them up, and soon Martha's little side had dots all over it from being squashed against the perforated grillework of the stroller.

It seemed we were the only ones out in Hillbank that evening, in the putrid sky, picking up elastic spools. I looked at Martha, very small beside the bulging bag. My mother, bending to the ground, didn't seem so big either. All three of us were caught up together in the huge yellow sky, so surrounded that we shrank to nothing. Elizabeth Anne was far away from my mother now. I was close as skin. Purgatory fire was bad but not completely bad.

Before she had her own baby, my aunt Fírinn came over on Saturdays on her way to confession. She often took me with her. We waited for the priest in the pews near the statue of Mary, pretty in her blue robes that flowed to the flickering lights at her feet. My aunt always gave me ten cents for a candle and let me light it. I watched it burn until a door opened and the priest rushed by us in his black dress. He never looked our way but walked straight into his polished wood box and turned on his light and waited. My aunt would get up and the other people who came early would get up and there would be a polite back-and-forth about places in line. Then one would push aside the thick curtain and the priest would sense a presence and turn out the light. I'd hear him slide open the grating through which my aunt Fírinn talked to him: "Bless me, Father, for I have sinned" is what she said.

The first time my mother took me to Mass was also one of the rare times she took me somewhere without Martha. I got to sit in the front seat of the car. The church was drafty and damp and crowded. We were late. My mother dipped her fingers into the font and blessed herself. I did the same. We tiptoed down the side aisle. My mother did a little half curtsey and knelt in the pew. We sat there in the shadows while the priest paced back and forth, talking in his strange magic language. My mother held her missal, a black book that dripped with shiny ribbons. She didn't look at it. She was silent until the priest knelt for the prayers after Mass and then her voice rose up shockingly in the direction of the Blessed Virgin as she rapped the front of her dress with a white-gloved fist, "O clement, O loving, O sweet Virgin Mary!" After Mass was over, my mother told me I could go to church by myself from now on—I knew the way and she had the housework to do.

At home, my father was lying on the couch with his eyes closed listening to the opera. His mouth opened in a smile when he sang out every little while. He was so happy. I felt sorry for him because he wasn't going to heaven. I asked him why the Jews killed Jesus. He said I was interrupting the music.

That night, my father came into my room and he saw me saying my prayers. He told me to get off the floor. He said it in a gentle way. He said he would teach me a prayer he had taught Elizabeth Anne so I wouldn't have to learn all that mumbo jumbo at church, adding that I shouldn't kneel because my knees were too bony and I would get splinters. He was nice to think of my knees. Then he began to pray a little at a time and I repeated:

"The Lord is my shepherd, I shall not want."

"The Lord is my shepherd, I shall not want."

"He maketh me to lie down in green pastures."

"He maketh me to lie down in green pastures."

"He leadeth me beside the still waters."

"He leadeth me beside the still waters." ...

When the prayer was finished, we were quiet for a while. My father got up to go. I caught on to his thumb and pulled. "Do you know any more prayers?" I asked him. He smiled kindly and he said a short one: "Now I lay me down to sleep, I pray the Lord my soul to keep. If I should die before I wake, I pray the Lord my soul to take."

When he kissed me good night, he looked over my shoulder, like he was looking for Elizabeth Anne. I looked too. She wasn't there, of course. And I was glad, but I knew he wasn't.

On Wednesday afternoons of my sixth year, I got out of school early so I could go to religious instruction. Sister Mary Augusta taught me catechism in preparation for first Holy Communion. Week after week, as I got deeper and deeper into the Full Story, I started to feel the weight of Elizabeth Anne's holiness. For she had become a child of God the night before she died. She had arrived before Him completely clean.

But I was still here long after my baptism, piling up sin after sin and surrounded by the near occasions of sin, my sister, Martha, and my mother. Martha especially became a terrible temptation for me. Every time I got near her, I earned another black mark. When we played cards, I'd fall over laughing if she picked up the Old Maid. She could never win a game because I cheated if I thought she might. I always made her be the cheese in "The Farmer in the Dell" and then I made fun of her standing all by herself. I called her Chubbette and told her there was a private bogeyman assigned just to her to wake her up and make her wet her bed. If she saw me slipping my meat into my napkin and told on me, I held a grudge against her, another sin.

My mother was an occasion of sin too. Every time I argued, another black mark. And all the time Sister Mary Augusta's voice echoed in my head: "Children who commit venial sins on purpose and do not try to do better will commit big sins when they grow up." If I didn't die before I got old, I would surely go straight to hell. I knew it.

Even after confession, my sins wouldn't be totally washed away because I would never be able to make a perfect act of contrition. I would ask forgiveness *chiefly* because I was afraid of the fires of purgatory, not because I loved God above all others. It would be like it was when I was polishing the silver. There would always be some black left to get off. Not only did Elizabeth Anne never polish the silver, she had her soul polished for her by the priest. And she didn't have Martha around.

I tried complaining to my aunt Firinn, but she brushed me off. She was so busy with her baby she only came over when my mother shut her door and wouldn't come out at all. One particular time, when the door finally opened, they both walked out as if they couldn't see me standing there. I went inside. My mother's bed was rumpled and I could see in the spread the print of her body. It looked as if a giant snail lived there, a big solitary snail. My father's bed was so neat. He hadn't been home for a long time.

My father said he wouldn't come to my first Holy Communion and anyway he would probably be traveling. I tried again. I stood near him when he played the piano. He liked Stephen Foster songs and I liked to hear his gentle voice when he sang, "Weep no more, my darling, Oh, weep no more today ... " I managed to get into his lap and so he stopped playing. I said: "Can I tell you what I've learned in religious instruction?"

"Don't you want to hear another song?"

"Yes, but could I tell you this first?"

"All right."

"It's about the miracle that happens at Mass. The Mass is really the same thing as the Last Supper except the priest takes the place of Our Blessed Lord. He has all the same power that God has. He says what Our Lord said at the Last Supper to make the bread change into His Body and the wine turn into His Blood. Do you want to hear what the priest says?"

My father's hands reached for the keyboard. I didn't have much time. "Hoc est enim corpus meum," I blurted, loudly.

"Oh, I know that." My father took his hands off the keys and held them in front of us, making a circle in the air with his thumbs and index fingers, as if he were holding up the Host. He said, "It goes like this, doesn't it—Hocus, pocus, dominocus. P.U. You stink!" He dropped his knees and slid me off his lap. I could hear the piano and his voice going gentle as I left him, singing about the corncob being ripe and the meadow filled with flowers and the birds making music all the day.

I wanted so badly to die before I woke, like in the prayer, and have the Lord take me to heaven. But it was too soon. I had to wait until my first confession or all my sins would travel with me. Maybe if I threw myself before a car on the way to church, my sins would be totally forgiven, the way God forgives people who die without baptism, as long as they have a desire to be baptized one day. But would God do that—because I would have planned to throw myself under a car before confession, and maybe planning was a sin. My enemy was my mind, always working against my innocence, always there to remind me I was a sinner in thought first of all—in word and deed, of course, but in thought most of all.

I finally made my first confession. It took a very long time. Afterward, Sister gave me a holy card with gold around the edges. It was a picture of Jesus with a crown of thorns on His head. I showed it to Julian Feinstein, who lived next door and was in the driveway shooting baskets. He asked me what I was and I said half Catholic, half Jewish. Then he asked me if I believed the Jews killed Jesus and I said yes, and Julian's mother said, "That's a shame."

There was a big surprise at home. My mother had straightened my room and was preparing it for my communion clothes. From underwear to gloves, all was new and very, very white. My veil was arranged over the lampshade. It had a satin ribbon sewn all around the edges. It was perfect. I was almost perfect. I had just worthily received the sacrament of penance and tomorrow I would receive Our Lord. "He who eats My flesh and drinks My blood abides in Me and I in him," I said very quietly to myself. Then I went to find my mother. She was in the basement ironing my white organdy dress. Her hair was up in pin curls and her face was covered with Vaseline to keep the dirt out of her pores. She said not to come too close because I would trip over the ironing cord. So I got Martha and ran a bath for us. Martha crouched in the back of the tub and kept cringing away from me, thinking I was going to try to put soap in her eyes, but I wasn't. I just washed her cheeks and a little on her neck.

Later on I heard a shrill noise coming from the kitchen, where my mother was arranging flowers. It was an alarming noise, very high-pitched and moving aggressively forward. I thought it couldn't be coming from my mother because she didn't make that sort of sound, a noise that ran away from itself, spiraling up out of reach and possibility, desperate, as if it knew it would fail but couldn't stop trying to get away, clean and free. I ran into the kitchen. "What is that noise," I demanded to know. And I was sorry as soon as the words were out because I knew the answer before she said it, too startled to be insulted: "I'm singing."

My father never saw me in my communion dress. I did get to be the first in the girls' line because I was the shortest, but my boy partner was ugly and he didn't have on white shoes like everybody else. The nun told him he had ruined his line. I felt ruined too. But then the lines parted as we got to the first pew and I genuflected well and fixed my attention on the altar. The priest took extra care with the words. When he turned to face us with the chalice, I was overcome with how near he was and how well I could see him. He was praying now, asking God to accept His Precious Blood as a sacrifice to redeem my sins: "Hic est enim Calix Sanguinis mei, novi et aeterni testamenti, mysterium fidei qui pro vobis et pro multis effundetur in remissionem peccatorum." Then he lifted up the chalice and I saw him drink the blood of Jesus Christ, the Son of God. I saw him swallowing it.

The railing had been opened specially for first communicants and we went up steps that normally only the altar boys used. I knelt with the others. The priest came down whispering to each one, "Corpus Domini nostri Jesu Christi . . . " I was on the end. When he came to me, I closed my eyes and put out my tongue. Nothing happened. I opened my eyes. He was staring into them. "So pretty," he said. He put the Host in my mouth and moved on. But had he talked to me in English, in ordinary words, words that don't come from Christ Our Lord? But *had* he said, "So pretty," like a man and not at all like Christ Our Lord? And where was God at this moment? Was He inside me the way He was supposed to be? Had I received the Lord and He me? Probably not. It probably didn't work if the words were wrong. In any case, I couldn't pray. I just stood there looking after the priest as he started in on the next group, " ... in vitam aeternam ... " There was a tap on my veil and a little push and I filed out and forgot to cross myself when I got to my pew.

I knelt very straight and buried my head in my arms and watched the light that came through the stained-glass windows onto the floor. I tried to count the motes that were moving through the beams. The light was soft and thick, the kind of light Elizabeth Anne probably played in, the kind of light in her hospital room, pale, touchable light.

I was already seven years old and I was still on earth.

My father came home late that night. In the morning he showed us a doll dressed in a beautiful slippery robe. Her hair was twisted on top of her head and she had red lips and white, white skin. He said she was a Japanese doll and that there were special women in Japan who painted their own faces white to look like her. The most beautiful women in the world were in Japan, he said. My mother said the doll's feet were too small, and then she remembered that I hadn't polished my shoes for school. We started arguing about when I would have to do that. Her voice got louder and she said, "Why can't you ever do the least thing without complaining, why do I have to tell you over and over again?" But by this time I was crying so hard I couldn't hear her, and I didn't even know why I was crying so hard except it was easier than talking, and anyway my father had left the room already so what did it matter. I started screaming any old thing, like "Martha doesn't have to do what I have to do, how come she gets special treatment?" Then I charged out of the living room past my mother, who said, "Don't you dare leave this house."

I slammed the back door as I left, running down the hill and through the fields across Maple Avenue. I kept going until I got to church and then I went around behind the back of the church, and I rang the convent bell and asked, "Please, could I see Sister Mary Augusta?"

She came into the room, surprised to have a visitor and not quite recognizing me—the way she always was with the public school kids. I had calmed down but I started up again to show her I was somebody to feel sorry for. She ran a finger underneath the white cardboard on her forehead and reached for her big black rosary. "Why are you crying?" she said.

I told her that my father wasn't going to heaven because he was Jewish and that my mother was going to heaven even though she didn't go to church because she had been baptized and her housework was church, and so was Martha, even though she was too little to go to church, and I was going—after purgatory, of course. "Everyone except for my father is going to heaven and he won't ever see Elizabeth Anne again because the Jews killed Jesus. The gates of heaven are closed forever to my father," I choked out. Sister Mary Augusta left the room and came back with a glass of water. She offered me her handkerchief and I wiped my eyes.

At first Sister didn't say anything. Then she asked me if I thought purgatory was going to be too hard for me and I said yes and I told her about wiping the black off the silver and how there was always some black left. She asked me if I knew what an indulgence was and I shook my head no and she began to instruct me:

"Indulgences are one of God's many gifts to His children. They work on our souls the way a washing machine works on our dirty clothes. They don't forgive sin, but they help clean away the stains that are still there even after the sin has been forgiven in confession. When was your last confession?"

"Saturday, before my first Holy Communion."

"Are you in the state of grace?" I hesitated. She asked again, "Have you committed any mortal sins?"

"No, Sister."

"You can earn an indulgence today. With these." She reached into her black skirts with one hand and with the other she reached for my arm. "Put out your hand," she said. She let fall into it a pale turquoise set of rosary beads, so beautiful I felt like I was in a fairy tale. "Do you know how to say the rosary?" she asked.

"Yes, Sister."

"Does anyone else at home?"

"I don't know. My mother's prayers are her housework and she is too tired at night to kneel down."

"In that case, you'll have to teach your sister. Because Our Lord has promised that if you say the rosary every day in the company of one other person, all the temporal punishment due for your sins will be taken away. You won't go to purgatory because your soul will be as clean as if it had just come out of the washing machine."

Then she gave me a tiny medal and said when the time seemed right I should ask my mother to sew it in my father's coat. After it was sewn in, I should say a thirty-day novena asking God to give him the gift of faith.

She was gently easing me to the door and I was saying "Thank you, Sister, thank you, Sister, thank you, Sister," and then I was outside and saying "Thank you, Sister" and running up the hill.

I was too scared to do anything about the medal for a long time. But I was crazy to start my indulgences. It was a big project. There were a lot of Hail Marys, fifty of them, and the Glory Bes and the Our Fathers and the immense Apostles' Creed, which Martha could never remember and always cheated on, making me furious in case that meant the indulgence was canceled.

But it was a rich life after that. So much to learn. So much to do. Indulgences completely preoccupied me. There was a partial indulgence for saying the prayer to my Guardian Angel in case we missed the rosary at night. There were partial indulgences for wearing an itchy brown scapular and for saying "My Lord and my God," and "Jesus, Mary and Joseph, I place my trust in you." I said these things tens of times. With my aspirations, I could shut out all the noise of dinner or make noise where there was nothing but painful silence, my mother with her elbows on the table, chewing gristle and saying, "Eat your meat." I said one when I knocked over her jelly-jar glass hidden under the skirt of the big chair and when I thought she might be coming up behind me while I was taking candy from the glass bowl in the dining room.

Indulgences really were wonderful, but I still would have preferred Elizabeth Anne's route to heaven, I told my aunt Fírinn when she came over one afternoon. She said that was a bad thing to say and I should go to confession and tell the priest. As it happened, it was a Saturday, and we walked down there together.

I took a tennis ball and chased it down the hill, bouncing it once in each panel of sidewalk, careful not to touch the lines and careful not to stop the rhythm by catching the ball. I lost control near the bottom of the hill. There was a car coming. I suddenly saw my chance and I darted into the street after the ball. My aunt Fírinn shouted after me. The car swerved with a hideous noise. The fender caught the hem of my dress and ripped it across the skirt, but I fell out of the way of the wheels.

My aunt and the driver were all over me. As soon as it was clear I was fine, my aunt pulled me up close to her and held me by the chin. "Don't you ever, ever, ever do that to me again. Even God will not forgive you if you go around scaring people like that. Do you understand me?"

The driver kept asking if I was sure I was okay. "I'm sure," I said, "I'm sure."

My aunt knew there would be trouble about my dress, so she had me change as soon as we got home and she hid it under her sweater. I kissed her and she nodded her head, accepting my kiss.

That night there was the usual silence at dinner. I looked over at Martha. She was singing all by herself. I couldn't hear the words, but it sounded so cute and it made me feel good. It was warm that night, for the first time that spring. I asked if Martha and I could go outside after dinner and my mother said yes, if we finished all our dinner. There was no chance of that. It was chicken soup with the fat riding on top. I was about to give up, but then I heard Martha still singing her little song and I remembered a funny face I had seen somebody make once.

"Watch me, Martha," I said and I blew one cheek out and then the other and then one cheek and then the other and then stuck my tongue straight out. Martha laughed, a big loud open laugh. So I did it again and I started to laugh too and then there were two girls together laughing their heads off at our kitchen table. And in the laughter was a wave of relief so powerful it was scary. Part of me fell into Martha's laugh and she was inside mine and the more we laughed the more our union grew until it became a solid, strong thing.

We probably sat there till it was dark, laughing out loud in each other's company until we couldn't laugh anymore. And I probably got Martha to eat my soup for me before we stole away to bed.

SAVING
THE
POOR

All my life I've wanted to fly, hoped I could fly, believed I could fly. Well, not always *believed*. That was only briefly when I was nine and *knew* it. All I had to do was practice and flying would come to me. I practiced by running down the hill in front of the house and leaping just before I got to the bottom. I practiced all spring after school in rain or shine until dinnertime. I swear there was at least one time I came close to succeeding—I had just the right combination of flapping arms and scissored legs in the air. It powered me past a yellow rosebush, a good seven feet from where I had taken off. I had to have been flying to get that far, I told my little sister, Martha, who asked my father if I was telling the truth, and he laughed out loud.

Flying stayed on as an idea in my head inasmuch as it represented the exotic to me. But the notion faded so much that when I received the booklet I had sent for about requirements for Pan Am stewardesses, I didn't look at it right away. When I did read it, I saw how tall stewardesses for Pan American had to be—over five feet two inches, I think it was. I was just ten and still growing, but height suddenly became the kind of insolvable problem everything was that year. I might grow, but I also needed glasses, and my father said my eyes would probably get worse the way his had, and my teeth would too, so what was the use.

I threw the booklet away, or lost it in the mess under my bed, where I tossed all the old *Reader's Digest* magazines with the stories about people who overcame their drinking problems and "you can too." Most of the stories were about men, though there was one outrageous tale by a woman who had faced the world sober after she lost her nose in a car accident because she was drunk. This woman was down on her luck. She had been fired for drinking and there was no hope of ever working again because she was really only good at darning socks, and socks had become cheap enough to throw away if they needed mending. At the end of her rope, she thought she might just as well drink herself to death at the local roadhouse. But she got so noisy she was thrown out, and that's when she hit another car and went through the windshield and sliced off her nose. A policeman came by and took pity on her and helped her up and fell in love with her, and the woman changed her mind about drinking herself to death and everything began to get better.

Whatever the drinking problem in a *Reader's Digest* story, the solution was always the same. Somebody had to fall in love with you. When I got to that part, I'd throw the magazine under the bed, knowing that even if my mother put her arms through the meat grinder she wouldn't stop drinking because, as she often told me, my father didn't love her. She was right. In our house, my father never called my mother "dear." He didn't kiss her unless he was going away on a long trip—at least I had seen it happen only that once when he went to Japan. He never asked her to try not to drink. When she bought a new dress, which was always too small and too frilly, he'd hold his nose with one hand and wave her away with the other. So it was no good hoping for my mother to stop drinking.

Even Bishop Fulton J. Sheen, who worked a kind of miracle in our house for a half hour a week, when we all sat close together watching him on television, couldn't make my father love my mother. Bishop Sheen got my father's respect although he had "juvenile Catholic ideas" because he spoke well of the Old Testament and appreciated humanism and most especially music. My father was drawn in by stories like the one about the missionary to the leper colony who slept in a piano box. It wasn't even a grand piano box. It was a box for an upright. And every night when the missionary climbed into his box and pulled up the hinged sides, he thanked God for his life and his home. "Not bad," my father would say. Then he'd jab his snoring wife and tell her to put away her darning and go to bed.

Something else happened around the time the Pan Am booklet came. I was on my way into the woods next to our house one misty afternoon. It must have been early in the spring because there were violets everywhere, but the ground hadn't completely thawed. There was an incline leading up to a big meadow.

I was looking down, cracking the thin ice over the mud holes with my shoe, so I was very close before I realized there was a man blocking my way to the meadow. He looked like he had come right out of the woods, as if he had slept in the oak leaves, and in fact there were oak leaves hanging from his shirt. He looked at me in a kind of pleading way and then gazed down. I followed his eyes and saw that his trousers were open. He started twirling his sex, fast and faster like a propeller blade. I couldn't take my eyes off it. It seemed I stayed there for a long time before I turned and ran.

Summer was almost over before I went past the entry into the meadow where he had stood and deep into the woods where the birch trees were and the wild iris and daffodil grew. The flowers were gone, of course, and I became glum and sad, swinging by one arm around the birch trees, knowing but not admitting, even to myself, that if I hadn't been so afraid I would have come back sooner. I went home and beat up my sister and told her she was fat and nobody liked her, and anyway she was adopted and as soon as winter came our parents were going to take her back out to the woods where they had found her and leave her there. She cried all night.

A little of the fight went out of me after that. I told Martha I was sorry, that it was really me who was the orphan, and that one day I was going to fly away, so she should be very nice to me from now on. I reinstated my practice afternoons, but I couldn't even get to the beginning of the bush. After a while I stopped trying, or stopped believing or hoping. I even stopped wanting to fly, and I missed that more than anything—the feeling of wanting something so much I would practice until I dropped to try to do it. In my heart now I knew I wasn't going anywhere. I started hitting tennis balls against the side of the house by the basement door.

In a sense I was wrong, because I did grow up and leave home and go to college and to Europe and arrive back in time for the sixties and marry a Boston Irish Catholic who could outtalk me and whose moral superiority was so overwhelming I could only be grateful he would let me have breakfast with him. Paul was a doctor, a general practitioner, and he was unequivocally clear as to his purpose on earth—to save the poor, or as he put it, "to practice medical and social justice." (It was from him that I first heard about the connection between health care and revolution—that health care was a right and not an economic privilege.) But in another sense I was dead right. A rough fear thickened inside me. In my mind, I never went anywhere new. In my mind, I played a game of tennis, hitting low ground balls inside the lines.

It was in that spirit that I chose the Domingo Valley desert in Arizona. Around the time Paul got the call to join the Great Society's Rural Community Services Project, I came across a story about agribusiness, about how the desert Southwest was becoming the vegetable garden of America. There was a picture of some fields taken from the air—row on row of pale green planted in giant square formations. It had a disquieting, military look to it, but it was still beautiful in its static way.

All around the green squares, there was the fantastic swirl and dip and loose curviness of untouchable desert. Then there were pictures of the houses of residents, groups of houses that looked like they had been built by the people who laid out the fields. There were thousands of people living in the houses, not hundreds of thousands, just thousands. Enough people for a dentist to care for, clearly enough for one who lived all by himself four days a week, commuting to Phoenix on weekends to be with his family. He had set up his practice in the desert valley because, as the only dentist for miles around, he told the reporter, all he had to do to make money was "answer the phone."

In the interview with the dentist, it came out that this

particular part of the Southwest desert was profoundly hostile country for human beings. A normal temperature in August was 120 degrees. The cattle feedlots made the air unacceptable by any standard. The drinking water had a high pesticide content. To this dentist, however, it was "worth living here, worth living in hell," if you could fly out, which is what he did. Fly out in his own airplane. There was a picture of the airplane too.

I thought that if we moved to hell, it would make me want to fly the way I used to want to fly. And so I told Paul when he was offered a choice of two posts—one in Mississippi and the other in Arizona—that I wanted to go to the desert. I remembered a photograph of my boy, Daniel, walking on the beach in Cape Cod, wearing one of his father's white T-shirts. He would be such a vibrant presence in the sweeping sand of western Arizona, I thought, like John the Baptist, the lone child who "grew and waxed strong in spirit and was in the deserts till the day of his shewing unto Israel."

I was very taken too with the idea of being part of the first contingent to do battle against the "growers," as I later learned agribusinessmen were called. Only the federal government could adequately protect the poor against regional social and economic discrimination. Only outsiders like us could help relieve the awful burden of the farmworkers' poverty. We would intervene in the cycle of ill health, unemployment and illiteracy with our new federally funded, small-scale, locally accountable health clinics and day-care centers. These last things are what Paul and I talked about, but what I thought about was this: it will be so hot it will burn my pants off and I too will fly out of hell.

We drive south from Phoenix, through Palo Verde, into the Domingo Valley desert. It's the day after Labor Day, 1969. The air starts to burn around Gila Bend. When we get to Domingo, the thermometer on Main Street says 128 degrees. Luckily the office is on the shady side of the street. Two guys are already there. Paul makes three and his brother Patrick, the lawyer, will be four when he gets here from Boston, in about a month.

We ask around and find out that the best housing, that is, the most reliable air conditioning, is in a project on the highway in Salcedo, a town that borders Mexico. No problem finding it. No problem renting. That's the beauty of living here. Never a line of people before you.

There's no doubt, however, that this is a truly inhospitable place. It feels like we are down deep here in the valley, way down in a sink hot as a furnace. There is a dizzying monotony to our housing complex—rows of units, all alike, all attached to each other, all facing other rows of units, all alike, all attached to each other.

Inside each unit are people who work either for the border patrol, whose job is to harass nonwhites, or for the Arizona Water Authority, which is the real power in the valley. The irrigation officials have more clout than the growers. They regulate the flow of water, say how much and when and to whom. Once they make a decision, there is no appeal, apparently, because they are backed by the opaque authority of technology and science. They are the reason there are no small farms here. A farmer with only a small piece of the desert couldn't afford to pay for the water even if the officials, who also set the price, were willing to let it flow his way.

Paul's job is to take the farmworkers' side—to fight any sign of discrimination and exposure to health hazards, and to lobby for new farmworker-controlled health services. So already we are at odds with our neighbors. We overlook this because of the strong and reliable air conditioning.

At first we are all alone. I think I am going to like that fine, and am surprised to find out how hard it is. Paul's work is slow, largely done one-on-one or in paper-filings about health conditions in the field. There are no demonstrations and no rallies, only meetings, for men only, at the Casa de los Amigos. Paul goes and hears José Hernandez, the community worker, give out the news about farmworker strikes in California and comes home all fired up for La Causa and Cesar Chavez. Cesar never comes to Arizona, but he might if we can get some real action going, something besides picketing supermarkets, which doesn't count because it's what we were doing back East.

I explore a little. Not much. Even when there's something, it's nothing, like the Orange Julius stand in the ShopMart parking lot. Nothing grows along the endless yards of concrete canals. And no birds. I can't seem to locate any clumps of people, no society. Maybe it's too hot. There is only the buzz of machinery in the day and at night the dreadful hot wind carrying feedlot dust and smells into every opening. This does not discourage me. I might feel out of place, but no one seems to belong here, the way people belong to other places, the way Paul, for instance, belongs to his neighborhood in Boston and to his Church and to his uncle, the priest, who talks incessantly on TV about him and his kind.

I covet Paul's history of belonging. His lineage is, as he says, "modest and pure." First came the cobblers and the clerks and later the lawyers and patriots, all of them hardworking people who died early and left a trail of rosaries and funny jokes. He has the eternal happy family, he likes to explain, bragging about the stout father who protects the delicate mother; the four brothers, who all wear the same size dress shirt, the father's size, and who sit around the fancy dining-room table eating ham and scalloped potatoes cooked by the chuckling maid and served by the frail mother, who wears a necklace to dinner and smiles round the table at her men in a coquettish way.

The truth is I decided on Paul when I met his mother, and I prayed she'd have me. It worked. Early on, I overheard a telephone conversation: "Paul's got a quiet one. She fits in." After that, it was only a matter of time before

Paul's uncle married us. Soon after, he came to our apartment. He admired the slogans painted on the walls in the fashion of the sixties, tributes to NO-GU-CHI, and to Rilke, "But Chartres was tall, taller, Angel, even than you," and he baptized Daniel in the name of the Father and of the Son and of the Holy Ghost.

The two of us, or rather the three of us, are the family now and our new town is at least a democratic place in terms of moral hierarchy. Everyone is a drifter here, everything is impermanent, except the irrigation system. And nothing, not even Paul's genetic spiritual excellence, is big or forceful next to that. I become rather bold and immodest in my daydreams of how I am going to change things, maybe learn Spanish really well and start the day-care center I talked about in Boston, maybe write tales of Mexican heroes for the schools here.

In only a few days, reality intrudes in a particularly nasty way. In my calculations before coming to the desert, I hadn't counted on, or had forgotten about, how afraid I am of bugs. It turns out we have arrived too soon—before, instead of after, the two-week cricket season in which they hatch and die. They do it all of a sudden and all together after the first rain. These are not ordinary green crickets that chirp in a wood. These are black, gushy bugs that hop and fly. I don't know all this until it's too late.

The sky clouds up one afternoon in late September and it rains, not very much. That evening we decide to go for a walk. I open the door and walk into a cloud of bugs. I keep walking. There are more and more and more. They jump in my hair, on my feet, on my arms. I scream and run back inside, slamming the door. I spray myself all over with bug killer and get into the shower and scream and cry and tear at my hair. When I calm down, I go look for Paul downstairs. He is reading Ivan Illich on poor people's diseases. "You'll feel better tomorrow," he says.

This starts a period of weirdness. I demand, and get from Paul, home delivery of meals from Orange Julius. When I hear a cricket in the house, I hunt it down and set up a watch. It swells and puffs out like a bellows, makes a black dirty noise, like it's trying to get into gear. Daniel picks up the dead ones and brings them to me like they're some sort of treasure.

Paul's brother Patrick and his wife Sheila and their twin sons arrive. Patrick gets right to work. Sheila decides not to be "an adjunct" to Patrick, so I stay home with impunity with her. I think I will do what she does, but then I can't figure out what it is she does, all day long. So mostly I sit around and smoke. I am amazed at how happy she is with her life, this round, blond California girl, pureeing carrots for the twins, swishing her Mary Travers hair to the beat of her whisk.

My sister, Martha, Daniel's godmother, visits a lot from Phoenix. We don't talk much. She is just back from getting a divorce in Reno, "six weeks in a Savon store" . . . buying and comparing nail products, "especially cuticle removers." We do the laundry together. Very soon we know the price and location of every item in the ShopMart. In the evenings, we all eat together. Sheila cooks. Martha and I do the dishes.

I do some sporadic picketing at Safeway, thinking this is maybe the way to start a day-care center, find women with children. It gives me a close-up look at the poor. Believe me, I don't think they know they are The Poor. They have such dignity. I mean, at least they know what they are doing. My last time on the line, I am carrying Daniel in my arms and he poops. I don't want to hold him like that, so when our line comes around to the front of the store, I go in and buy a pack of diapers.

I tell Paul I am having trouble finding my place in all this, about how the poor don't look the way I thought they would look. For once, I have his full attention. I say I don't think I can go on unless I have some purpose here.

"What do you mean, 'can't go on'"?

"I mean any day now I could melt into the ground."

"You better stop talking like that. You're going to ruin the marriage."

We are so surprised by this conversation, we pretty much stop looking at each other, pretty much stop everything personal between us.

Daniel and I are together in our aimlessness. His cousins are contemplative, contented babies, and Daniel doesn't like them. He pulls their hair to make them stand up. One day, after he's gone too far, I pack him up and some pots and some pans and wooden spoons and set out on the highway. I have in mind the BIG sandbox, the dunes surrounding the mountain on the border. I turn off the main road and start in on the sand roads, following one that wiggles a kind of funny way. In less than a minute, the car is half buried. I think there must be some mistake, sand is good for traction. We get out of the car. I tell Daniel to play, but he balks. It's awfully hot, and he wants to go home. I pack the car, take a clean diaper, pick up my mass of a boy and start walking.

The sun begins to set, but incredibly fast. I think I see a shortcut straight to the highway across the dunes. But it isn't a shortcut. I hadn't realized how hilly the sand was. I must have been on a dune when I glimpsed the asphalt, because I lose it very soon and besides that I keep sinking in animal holes up to my thighs. Every fifteen minutes or so, we come up again and I see the highway, the cars going home, and I wave the diaper and yell "Help." Daniel starts to yell, too, and that scares me more than anything. He really means it. We get to the highway way after dark and I thumb a ride. The man who picks us up does public relations for the growers, our enemies. He also teaches flying. By the time we get home, he's going to teach me, starting tomorrow.

The air is still impossibly dry and the morning sky still blinding white and the valley floor is still flat and green and brown. But all of a sudden I can take it. In fact I fly with it. I live for takeoffs, for the moment speed conquers gravity and we lift off the ground. Soon nothing feels better to me, has ever been better, than a midair stall. I love nosing up into it. I love the buzz before the engine fails and then the silence and then the spin of the plane as it spirals down and down and almost too far down. I always get us out of the spiral. My instructor is pleased, sitting there beside me, hands off the controls.

There is controversy at home about this new development, but it's minimal. "Airplanes are elitist. . . . The growers own airplanes. . . . " I ignore these remarks. It's so long since conversation has been direct that it's easy to let slurs go. Our lives are still more or less going in the same direction. No need to cause any ripples. I'm still on the right side. After all, I'm not going to own a plane. I'm just going to fly one.

"Fly it where, do what—deliver mail?" Paul wants to know.

"Maybe."

To soothe my conscience I undertake to instruct my instructor in the evils of the system, how the growers use the technocracy of the Water Authority to squelch any movement toward small farm cooperatives, how they perpetuate the system of capitalist exploitation of poor people who have no choice but to accept their terms or go away.

At night I borrow Patrick's Austin Healy and drive. I

take it out past the mountain where Daniel and I were stranded, straight on the highway till the highway winds into desert mountain, heading deep into the desert, to the rock country past the dunes. I kill the motor when I get high into the rocks. Some nights the stars are so bright and so near. They cover me like a bowl. I think about nothing when I take Patrick's car out into the night. It is so clean out there. And quiet. And there are the rocks and the stars, and the eerie, eerie light of nothing in my way.

Patrick and Paul are getting famous. Paul is such an implausible radical, a tall softy with long arms and two big freckled hands, one around a glass of milk and the other full of Fig Newtons. He's a good decoy for Patrick, the small, muscular one with good teeth whom the priests beat up in high school and who gave them the finger behind their backs. The office has so many suits and petitions for health services going that the newspapers can't keep up with them. The boys have to be clever to get them because the poor don't give a hoot about fighting discrimination. The only thing anyone really wants is a divorce. The brothers are a real team with a case like that. They know what goes on in the mind of a man who wants to commit sacrilege—to tear apart what God has joined in the holy sacrament of marriage.

They can spot a target a mile away, someone wearing a scapular over a buttoned-up short-sleeved shirt. His wallet is full of holy cards and pictures of the family. The brothers admire these and listen attentively when the man tells them he will settle with God later. Now he needs a divorce.

Paul leads. He talks very fast about the personal effects of discrimination, about a poor person's right to paved roads and streetlights and working sewers and telephone service, about how true unhappiness and ill health spring from being paid lower wages than whites or from not getting a job at all because a man isn't white. He tells of a way such hideous injustice might be ended, a legal matter involving the man putting his name to a lawsuit on behalf of all his people who suffer the indignity of discrimination in the valley or whose only hope of obtaining medical care is to become an emergency. His signature, his lone signature, could smash the racial barrier once and for all.

The man sits, hands folded prayerfully in his lap, his mind numb and uncomprehending. After a while Patrick breaks in with the only full sentence he knows in Spanish: "Sir, tell me, a shadow has come between you and your wife?" The man, after a moment, blinks yes. Patrick elbows Paul. "We must help him," he says, and draws up divorce papers.

With so many divorces, they quickly find plaintiffs for their suits and pile up enough affidavits about inadequate or unavailable medical treatment to petition for federal funding of a farmworkers' general medicine clinic to be run by a board dominated by farmworkers.

The clinic, or the idea of the clinic, causes a real ruckus in the valley. All the doctors and hospital workers are against it. They say it isn't needed, that it's socialized medicine, that it's being pushed through without consultation with them and that it's sponsored by militants and Communist agitators. The county officials say the clinic will encourage migrant workers to stay in the valley past the time they are useful and become a burden to the taxpayers.

But the federal government comes through and sends $285,000. The county brings suit, asking for an injunction to hold up spending the money, but the judge rules for the clinic. This causes enough excitement for Cesar Chavez himself to say he's coming for the opening ceremonies.

My instructor schedules me to solo for the first time the day of the dedication. He knows I can't make it, that I must be there to see Cesar. We argue. He says he doesn't give makeups, especially for the reason I'm giving him—to see that fraud.

"So you wait a week to go up alone. What's the difference?" Paul says.

At the dedication, the priest wears a shiny emerald-green surplice. The altar boys ring chimes and carry lighted candles. They follow the priest through La Clínica de Campesinos, a freshly painted trailer with minimal equipment—a dispensary table, basic medical instruments, scales, boxes of gauze and an oversupply of disposable hypodermic needles. The priest speaks in Latin to the supply cabinet, sprinkling drops of holy water as delicately as if he were blessing a newborn baby.

Outside everyone gathers for the speeches. Several hold up the farmworker flag, a bright red-and-black warning to no one in particular. Children wear homemade signs: SALUBRIDAD! VIVA LA RAZA! VIVA LA CAUSA! A lady in a big hat with a *Huelga* button, a pink feather and a small picture of Jesus on it tells about the nosebleeds, headaches, blisters and sore lungs she got from pesticides. She talks about the fields with no toilets and about how the fight for the dignity of the manual worker mustn't end with her generation but go on to the next and the next.

Overhead, there is a faint whirring sound. It's a biplane turning the corners of a nearby produce field, loosing a fine white mist over the crop. Daniel sees it too. "Pretty. Bird," he says.

There is singing for the first time since we've been here. I finally learn the words to "We Shall Overcome" in Spanish.

Cesar stands alone, a little apart with his dogs all around him. He is weak from fasting and maybe from the threats on his life. His black hair hangs over his eyes, only partly shielding him from the punishing sun. When the singing stops, he moves to the podium. He gives a short speech, reminding us he is one with us. Then he reports on the strikes in California, stressing the importance of nonviolence. He's smart about the picket line. It's a beautiful thing, he says. A man makes his commitment to the strike and to nonviolence on the picket line. It's where he learns that it's better not to have a gun, to make the other guy have the hard decision. It takes the fear away, he explains.

After the speeches, the kids look around for a place to hang the piñatas. José Hernandez, the community worker, climbs in the back of a pickup and holds up one for the children, who poke at it with a car radio aerial.

Paul and Sheila take the children home. I drive Patrick in his car. I don't remember being alone with him before. Must be the first time. My tongue is loose in the hot wind. I keep up a monologue of stuff—I don't know where it all comes from. I tell him about how I always wanted to fly, and this is my chance, and about how well I'm doing, and so what if it's the other side that's teaching me—I'm not going to fly a crop-duster even if it is the most elegant small plane around, and the most graceful. After all, I'm not out to kill anybody. And what about Cesar anyway, he's so easy on the pesticide issue. He knows how many workers are maimed and dying or close to dying from those poisons. He also knows something else. He knows that if he really attacked and exposed the magnitude of the problem, he'd drag the whole farm industry down with him. And then where would his people be? Nowhere, starving nowhere, that's where . . .

We turn into our row. I hand over the keys as I get out of the car. Patrick catches my skirt. "Just a minute," he says, grabbing my head. His hands cover my ears. He kisses me once, quickly. Once again. His mouth is in my ear and he hisses: "You're afraid of the airplane, aren't you? You're afraid to take off alone. Afraid."

I run inside and upstairs. Paul is already sleeping. I shake him and tell: "Do you know what your crazy brother just did, your crazy brother just kissed me." Paul rolls away toward the window. I repeat myself and shake him a little more. He doesn't hear me, though he hears me. I stop shaking him.

In the morning, I cross the lawn with Daniel to Patrick's house. He's reading the paper, offers us some toast. It's as if nothing at all has happened. Daniel and I walk out and over to the Circle K. We sit on the stoop eating powdered doughnuts.

A few nights later we are playing bridge. Patrick's hand is suddenly on my knee. "Two clubs," he says. This goes on for weeks. Now I am the one setting up bridge games. Once I go down to the office to bring in a patient needing a ride. Patrick wants to come out for lunch. He follows me, slips his hand down the back of my skirt. I lean into his hand.

There is a series of brief, private encounters—in a child's room, in his car, on circular steps. They are very sudden, over very suddenly. Mating takes seconds.

Mostly, there are long, long spaces of time. Unseemly yearnings to be touched, to be talked to, for him to brush past me in a knowing way. I wake up hopeful with the morning light, walk out by the levee where the earth is cracked and wrinkled and the canal is grungy with silt and salt. Somehow the day goes by. I have the habit of it.

Take a matchbook. Tear it into little bits, smaller bits, smaller and smaller. One by one a bit is gone. There are events. The mailman. A magazine. Daniel's lunch. The afternoon walk to ShopMart. The discussion about toilet training with the French wife of the border-patrol officer next door. The evening walk to the levee. Answering the phone. It isn't the phone. It's my ears. Once I meet my flying instructor in the supermarket. "Come back and fly," he offers.

"My husband says no."

At night, Daniel sleeps. Paul reads. I take the car and Patrick, if he will come. Not often. Then late, late back from the rocks. Sometimes Patrick leaves his light on. That is, once he leaves his light on.

We sit in the spare room, me on top of Patrick's crossed legs. We rock back and forth, his tongue in my ear, my head in his neck. The sky is light for nighttime. Nothing matters to me now. Nothing matters except I am rocking on Patrick's crossed legs. I have a feeling of being saved, as if somebody said, "Put an umbrella over that girl's head." And he did it. For a moment. Yet I feel sure that I am rocking toward the center of evil. And soon I will know exactly what evil is. I mean I will know for sure, because I really know already.

Evil is rocking. Evil is deception, a lullaby. Evil is a

lullaby, rocking, rocking until you know you are cared for, until you are perfectly sure of it, can hold on to it, describe how it feels like being saved, so sure of it you can close your eyes and think: I have found the one who owns me, who owns me so completely he can never be separated from me, can't ever leave me, must love me from now on, always love me, rocking back and forth, loving rocking, loving me. Evil is when you open your eyes and there is nothing there.

Except this time, there is. Something there. Something out there on the grass, coming across very, very slowly. It is very, very large, like a ground cloud, a big white puff coming toward me at a slow majestic pace. Instead of growing larger though, it gets smaller, as if my past were coming toward me, and my past were a sack of dreams emptying itself onto the ground. The figure is near now and so shrunken that it barely covers my knees when I stand before it. I slide open the glass door. Daniel is in the path of a moonbeam, his diaper falling down, big white T-shirt hanging off one shoulder, lips wet and trembling. We stare into each other's eyes. I stare into my past and he stares back into his future.

"Hi, Mom," he says.

SISTERS

□ □ □
□ □ □

The first phone call came in the afternoon. I was filling in an application for my husband to be a medical school professor. In the last days of the Great Society, some of the big universities recruited young doctors out of rural clinics to teach its students community health care. They called it Poor People's Medicine. If Paul and I went back East, it would get us out of the Arizona desert and away from his older brother. I just couldn't stay away from Patrick anymore, unless I *was* away. It was as simple as that.

Anyway, the phone rang and it was my sister, Martha. She was excited. She said she had just had a chase in the parking lot of her building complex outside Phoenix. A man with a gun had chased her. What did he want? I asked. He wanted me, she yelled. Why? Don't you know anything, she said and then she hung up. I called right back and she said there was a pounding on her door. I said, Call the police, but she wouldn't get off the phone. She just started crying in this kind of stringy, helpless way, and so I ran across the grass into Sheila and Patrick's house and picked up the phone and called the Phoenix police. "Don't sweat, ma'am," said the officer on the line, "we'll get to her." I was frantic by then, so I called the office. Paul wasn't there, but Patrick was, and he said, "It's okay, I've got a friend in Phoenix, I'll take care of it." Patrick can do anything.

It turned out to be a big fuss for nothing. The pounding on her door went away, the police came, and Martha gave them some of her really good fudge she makes from scratch.

But that was the beginning. Martha called at every odd time of the day or night. It was always something out of the blue. She wanted to know if I remembered which one of us Dad used to pick up first when he came in the door after work. Or did I know about this research that said people who are brain-damaged in a certain part of the brain can't understand pronouns. "They can say everything else, but they don't know who is who in a sentence like 'I love you.'" Once she wanted to know if she could send her white alpaca coat to the cleaner's.

It was all stuff that had boiled over from the year she lived in Ottawa, married to Jim. He found her bankbook on their honeymoon, and he told her he had married rich, but not rich enough. She brooded about that for a year while she vacuumed her apartment. Then she went to Reno and got a divorce. She didn't tell me what went wrong until it was all over. We don't talk about money in our family. We just have it. That is our father has it, someplace far away safe, someplace where he is, away from our mother. He took back Martha's bankbook, and I've never seen mine. I'll probably never be old enough, and Paul didn't strike him as old enough either, which surprised me, because I thought any male was old enough.

Martha's calls were a salvation for me in a way. They took my mind just slightly away from Patrick. I stopped plotting quite so much to see him and began relying on chance, since, in fact, he was almost always around at night and in the day, of course, he was too busy for me. They worked like demons under Patrick's direction in the Rural Community Services Project, collecting evidence for "landmark" poor people's cases, pressuring for more jobs or better conditions in the field or federal money for dental clinics and health clinics and day-care programs. They had these big, important meetings about strategy: how to beat the growers at their own game; whom to support—the people crossing the border for jobs, or the people who were already union and on strike against the growers. I don't know where they got their points of view or how they could live with themselves when they totally changed their minds and went back on what they had been arguing for days at a time. When I sat in on these debates, I always wanted to ask, From where does your authority come? What do you really know how to do? But of course I never did say anything because I was too busy making sure Patrick sat next to me. He always reacted if I could get close enough. A single brush against him and I could be sure he'd take me home by way of the dunes.

Thanksgiving night I heard Patrick tell his brother he was going to drive to the border to watch the predawn traffic of illegals. I sat up all night waiting for his light to go on, and at around four I got dressed and was outside when he opened his door. When we got there, I joined the picketers—against the growers, I think it was, or maybe the union. Patrick and I drove home together and we parked briefly somewhere in nowhere. I lay down for him. The desert here is beautiful and bare, and daybreak is like a windowshade going up all around at the slowest possible speed. As usual, we didn't talk, except this time he said, at the worst possible moment, "What do you think Paul would think of you now?"

On the way home to Salcedo, I asked him, "Why did you let Paul marry me?" But he didn't know what I was talking about.

When we got back, Paul was awake with Daniel, who had gotten up early and emptied a milk carton on the kitchen floor. The phone rang and it was the hospital where Martha worked—she teaches speech in the nursery school for disturbed children. Martha's supervisor said that Martha had come to work but was in no condition to work, and wasn't I her nearest relative, and could I come up right away? I said I would be there in four hours, which is what it takes to mop the kitchen and drive out of the Domingo Valley desert to Phoenix.

I got there in no time, it seemed. Martha was in the corner of the office of her supervisor. She was hiding, the way she used to as a kid. She was sitting in a ball with her knees covering her face and hugging herself and swaying. I said, "Martha, what is it?" and she didn't answer. I knew she wouldn't. The supervisor had already made an appointment with a doctor who lived an hour and a half away. She showed me the way on a map. It's a testament to how scared I was that I actually understood and didn't seek refuge in incompetence. On the way Martha stayed in her little ball except once she opened the door. We were going seventy-five and I was trying to switch lanes. I don't know how we got there, but we got there and then Dr. Beckman met us at the door and told us to wait. I couldn't believe it. I couldn't wait another moment. I had never seen Martha so difficult.

But we waited. I took her outside to the driveway, which was full of tiny powdery stones; the colors looked like Jordan almonds but the shapes were all different. We sat down and spread our legs as if we were about to play jacks but instead I started picking up the stones and letting them fall slowly, and Martha started doing the same thing. A peace came over us.

Then Dr. Beckman came out and said Martha should come with him. I got up too and pretended I had something important to do, like look at the trees. As soon as they went inside, I sat back down in the driveway and sifted stones.

In no time, it seemed, Dr. Beckman motioned me to come in. He showed me into a parlor where he wrote out a prescription for Martha. I didn't know where Martha was, and I didn't want to know. I was dreading being alone with her.

Dr. Beckman said that the pills would take a few weeks to work, to "stabilize" Martha, and that I should bring her back after the first of the year and they would start therapy. I told him about Martha opening the car door and he said he would tell Martha not to do that again. I wanted to ask if we could spend the night, but of course I didn't, and then Dr. Beckman opened the door and there was Martha standing up by the window, smoking a cigarette and holding a fresh one in her other hand.

"Martha, your sister is waiting for you," Dr. Beckman said gently, and we were gone.

I had in mind to drive straight home, but we had to get the prescription filled. When we got to the mall, Martha said her cleaning was ready and she must pick it up. It was the first thing she had said all day. I told her the cleaning could wait. I went around to open her door and took her by the hand and we went into the drugstore. The pharmacist said it would take an hour. "She's very sick," I said. "Could you give her something now?"

"Who's sick?" he asked, and I turned to show him Martha and she wasn't there. I panicked then. I told the pharmacist to get my package ready immediately or I would get the police, and I ran around and around the pharmacy calling out for Martha. I scoured the parking lot and then I went back and picked up the prescription and the pharmacist said, "You can't fool me, lady. You're the crazy one." I got into the car and turned on the radio, and started crying because I couldn't stand the thought of how many more years I had left of sleeping next to a man with big freckled hands who always smelled like Fig Newtons, even after he showered. I remembered it was Martha who first noticed the freckles.

Pretty soon Martha knocked on the window and made a motion to open the trunk. She was carrying plastic bags full of white garments. Her cleaning. I was so mad I made her take two pills and we drove straight out of Phoenix. Near Cholla we stopped and had some pancakes, though neither of us ate much—we've always been competitive noneaters.

It was late when we got home. Paul was in bed, but Patrick was up, and he came over when he saw the headlights turning in on the Verde Park Estates sign. He was cuddling a beer to his chest and he offered it to Martha.

She took it. The Circle K was still open, so I left them alone for a minute and went over and got some Ripple. That's the only thing that tastes good to me. It works fast too. When I got back, Patrick was standing over Martha as she undid her hair—it's long and chestnut, and it gets messy if she doesn't braid it. I didn't like the way he was looking at her. I said I was going to put Martha to bed and I'd come over later. He said he was so beat, he'd have to sleep soon, and he'd see us tomorrow. Usually that would have really rattled me—I would have sat up all night waiting for morning. But I was tired, so I just walked him halfway across the lawn and put my hand in his back pocket and squeezed and he smiled and I said bye.

I was up early finishing Paul's application. I gave it to him to mail. Then I had him take Daniel over to Mama Linda's Daycare. I told Daniel I would pick him up when Martha felt better. How do you know how she feels, she's asleep, Daniel said, not unreasonably.

I never have had the feeling my son is on my side.

Martha came down a few minutes later carrying all her clothes and the sheets from her bed and wanting to know where the laundry room was. She really likes to do the washing. When we were kids, she always picked it. That left me with floors, but sometimes I could get her to do those too, between loads. Anyway, I gave her my laundry too and we walked over to the laundry room. We didn't speak at all, except I told her not to throw away the odd

61

socks and to act normal around Daniel because I didn't want him to be frightened of my family. She nodded as if she was taking that in.

Around noon, she mixed up some baby oil and iodine in a baby bottle and took one of the clean towels and laid it on the grass. It was over 110 degrees out there, but she didn't seem to notice. She just smoothed herself all over and held up the bottle to me—she knew I would be watching her from inside. I pushed away the glass door and screen and went out to her. She cried when she felt my hand and shuddered and dropped to the ground and was asleep immediately. She had some beautiful body. It was amazing. That former little Chubbette, grown into a stunning thing. I have no idea what a lioness looks like, other than a big cat, and Martha didn't really look like a big cat out there, but she did look like a lioness.

Paul came home to eat. The table is right by the glass doors, so we stared at Martha all during lunch. Paul doesn't like conversation while he's eating.

"What's wrong with her?" he asked after he finished off the last of the cookies.

"She wants to kill herself."

"Why?"

"She thinks she'll never have a boyfriend."

"So?"

"So, it's like Dylan says, 'Love is all there is.'"

He just looked at me then—something rare—and put some zinc oxide on his lips and all over his nose and went

back to the office. Fair skin and hair the color of canta-
loupe are not grounds for divorce. Why had I married a
perfect man?

Martha slept, and I listened to Dylan all afternoon.
When I went to get Daniel and we came back from the
grocery store, she was back upstairs in bed. Things sort
of went along like that for a couple of weeks. Martha
hardly ever broke her silence. She shuffled the first week,
as if she were crossing an ice pond on double runners.
Gradually she began to bend her knees. We got her to
play bridge sometimes, but not any tennis. Mostly she just
sat and smoked. I washed her hair almost every day. I've
always liked to do that. When I rubbed her scalp she
uncurled her fingers, like one of those African plants that
opens when it's touched. Every now and then she'd start
to dial Mom back East, but I kept reminding her about
how useless it would be. My mother keeps a clean house,
no bugs anywhere, but she drinks all day and complains
about us girls. We don't clean properly, she says, and we
won't succeed if we can't master the basics. None of my
father's women even makes the bed, but I can't tell Mom
that. She wouldn't get it anyway.

I did worry some about Patrick and Martha. She was,
after all, so silent and beautiful. And I'm ashamed to admit
it, but I tracked her every move.

I figured it started on the day Martha turned twenty-
two, but I've never known exactly. That was a Saturday.
Patrick was outside fooling around with the engine on his

car. I was watching him through the glass doors while I made a cake. I had a Betty Crocker booklet that showed how to cut up cakes into different animals. I was making a giraffe. Martha wasn't interested because the icing was caramel-flavored. Neither one of us really likes caramel— I just needed to make it that way for the color. She went on outside. I thought I saw the two of them exchange one of those looks my father sometimes gave my mother on Sunday after dinner, something pretty fierce and quick, signaling a transaction absolutely exclusive to them. I decided the sun was playing tricks on me and I kept stirring. But pretty soon I couldn't stand not knowing. Patrick had suddenly disappeared from my line of sight too.

I found Martha right away folding socks in the laundry room. She was serenity itself and she had obviously been at this for a good while. She had the socks in a long line, all neatly stretched out. She was going through the line slowly, picking out one pair at a time and taking the pair over to a separate table nearby. She worked her hands through each sock to make it even neater, pressing it down with her palm. Then she put them together, made sure they were pulled to exactly the same size, and then with a quick, violent twist, she tied them in a knot. I went back to my cake and cut out legs for the giraffe.

On Christmas Martha cried, starting early in the day, and I had to keep her in her room because she was spoiling it all for Daniel. The next morning I gave her a real good talking-to and said she'd have to shape up because she would be here for two more weeks and she was making trouble. She packed her bag and walked out the door with her good clothes on hangers and still in the cleaner's bag. We had a fight then. I scratched her arm badly with a coat hanger. We stopped when we saw the blood. I got out things to clean her up and I started talking, mostly to myself, but it worked to calm us both.

I told her all about Patrick, about how it started when he grabbed my skirt, about how after that it seemed like accidents. (Was it really accidental that time he put his thumb on the inside of my wrist, is there any other way to hand over a tennis racket?) At first I'd forget about him when he wasn't around, but then, I don't know why, I started thinking about him all the time, and then I started waiting for him, and I was still doing that. Now I waited for Martha to sleep before I snuck out to see if I could get him to come for a ride with me. I told her how my body was nothing but a shell to house this monstrous desire I had for Patrick, that I was all desire, and except for taking care of her and Daniel, which I really wanted to do, take good care of her especially, I was nothing else. I told her how Patrick blinded me when he wanted me. It was such a relief to be wanted, such an abrupt change, though it was sort of brutal between us now. The time had passed when I could hope he would lift my skirt and kiss my knee, so to speak. Now whatever happened, happened in a small, animal way. Yet he had come to be the

65

only thing that counted for me, the only thing to be considered. Only Martha could have interrupted it, and I was glad she had because now I could see how much I wanted them both, Patrick *and* Martha.

"What about Sheila," she wanted to know.

"I think Sheila knows," I told her. "I don't think she cares. All she wants to do is make soup. She cooks soup all day long for those twins."

"You always hear what you want to hear and see what you want to see. I thought you cared about this family."

"I do care about this family. That's why I want you to get better. So you can be part of it. So I'll have somebody on my team."

"I have to check the laundry. I think I left my pink shirt in the dryer."

"Why are you always doing laundry? What is so dirty, Martha?"

But she was gone.

I had shocked her, of course. I could tell I had. I had always been the one in charge of our moral development. I made us say the rosary every night. I dictated how fast, how slow, whether silent or out loud, and said whether it was a race or not. I heard her confessions before we walked down to Holy Name on Saturday afternoons. I was the one who decided whether it was her fault or mine that our mother cried that week. I always made her repeat her penance to make sure her sins were really washed away.

Then when we were older, I lectured her on the forces of diminishment, by which I meant our home, the routine boredom there, brought on by ... God knows what; could the enmity between our parents produce such a poisoning chill? Who could know? The important thing, I told her, was to escape. Because what was truly impossible to reverse was the loss of the world through some inward withering, some gradual diminishment of the soul. At all cost, she and I were going to avoid that. I promised her we would avoid it by leaving.

Now I kept on saying whatever was on my mind. For example, I told her I could understand why she wanted to kill herself, because she didn't have what I had with Patrick. I figured she was tuned in now and, sooner or later, she'd have to respond, and she'd have to help me keep us all together. It was all we had really. I could tell she was getting ready to give up and say she wanted to go back East to Mom, where you never knew night from day, it was all so much the same. Clean and drink, drink and clean. I couldn't let her go.

I said that if she'd just get better, I'd bring in one of the other two brothers, Brendan, or Brian. Probably Brian. He was still in medical school, but he'd be out soon, and they'd be perfect together. She'd have Brian and me and this family and we'd build a new unit. "We have to stick together and we have to stick to this new family. How else are we going to be saved?" I reasoned to her.

On New Year's Eve, we decided to go across the border to Fortunato to have dinner and dance. I dressed Martha in a blue mini that only just covered her fanny and I wore my tie-dyed T-shirt that clung in a way I knew Patrick liked. I told Martha to practice being self-confident by dancing with Paul, practice for when she would be with Brian.

Martha came down the stairs and ran right into Paul, who was cleaning his glasses and had his head down. "Whoa," he said, "let me look at my little sister." Martha kissed him on the ear. "Ah, she loves me. Just like all the girls," he said. "In the end, all the girls love me."

New Year's Eve in Fortunato was totally festive. We all danced in a madcap way. I love those mariachi bands, and there was confetti, and everybody laughed and hooted and shouted things I didn't understand and it was fun. When I looked in the mirror in the ladies' room, I was smiling so broadly I didn't recognize myself. Patrick wanted to know if I wanted another Marguerita. Oh no, I said, it must be time to go home. I looked around for Martha. She was dancing with Paul. She was smiling but she wasn't talking. There was something really creepy in her smile.

There was a little mix-up when we got outside. Martha ended up in the Austin Healy with Patrick. I was disappointed, but really I was too high to get worried. I took the baby-sitter home and when I got back, all the lights were out in both houses.

I sat outside for a while on the stoop. There was a hot

wind, the kind I would never have believed existed when I lived in the East. Wind was always mean and cold then. Now wind was always warm. I stretched my legs so it could get in under my knees. The sky was deep blue and every single star was there.

I don't know how long I stayed that way. When I crept back inside past Martha's room the light was already coming in through the window. I heard a little gasp, and suddenly there was Martha bolt upright on her mattress, facing down the most enormous waterbug I had ever seen. Martha, even more than I am, is afraid of bugs.

That's it, I thought, that's the end. She'll go now.

And I was right, because that evening Martha came down with her bags packed and her cleaning still in the plastic and asked for a ride to the airport. She was going back East to Mom.

More than a year passed before I found out what really happened to send her away. Paul and Daniel and I were in France by then. I wrote her to ask her to come, and to say Paul and I were separating—he was going back to Boston to do a residency in ophthalmology and I was staying in Paris to finish my degree in art history—and that still Patrick was the only thing on my mind after her. After all the wine and the whole length and breadth of the Louvre, he was still the only live thing in me.

And she wrote back, out of sympathy and trying to touch me where it could help. She said she knew how I felt but not to put myself down for it. She said, "What we felt for Patrick was primitive and basic, a thing that happens when a human being is bored and starving." And "Besides," she went on, "who else ever cared about us. Whoever else thought we were desirable. Put it that way."

□ 5 □

COMMUNION

□□□

Father Dwyer? So early in the morning. I can't even count straight yet. Why do you come? There's nothing new.

Let's begin.

It's finished, Father. It's over. I haven't had a drink for ages. You know that.

Let's begin.

You're kidding. You can't reach me anymore, you ghost of a thing. I don't even have any.

There's brandy in your riding boots. The right one. Go get it.

No.

Let's begin.

Okay. So you want to hear our story again. All right. I've got the time. But I'm not drinking.

We'll get to that. Begin.

So I am eight and I am still in ankle socks. I am among the public school kids, waiting for the Holy Name school to let out so I can come in for religious instruction as I do every Wednesday. You are there in the schoolyard. I can see the outline of your legs through your black skirts as you move over your turf, cuffing the bad boys, training your eyes on the sloppy girls filing past you. Reflexively, they tighten their knees, throw back their shoulders and lower their gaze. Like them, I am afraid of you, but I know you care about your charges. And so I want to be one of them.

But you never even nod to us outsiders, rising up and down on the balls of our feet behind the iron gates. To you, we are heathen, untamed children, suspect because our parents don't have the wit to put us in uniform and send us to your parochial school, where you could beat the knowledge of God into us. Chewing on our braids, scuffing our shoes on the pavement, deliberately breaking the code of modesty by staring into your deep, deep eyes, we are the type who probably comfort themselves at night with their hands between their legs. But we will never tell you this. We don't even know that such comfort offends God, whom we are not worthy to know. That's how ignorant we are.

You never had the innocence of my children.

Innocence comes from others. You would not think of me as innocent.

You never had their restraint, their tenderness.

I have the qualities you gave me. I am your creation, your dream of me. It is your idea that I not fit in with the obedient, quiet girls. You yourself ensure this. Early on you separate me and you keep me apart. In the confessional, you call me by name, refusing me even the pretense of anonymity. You talk about my hair when you are supposed to be giving me communion, leaving me speechless. I cannot blend into the prayerful murmur of the others, Amen, Amen, Amen, and I do not pray at all.

Still, I want you to love me, so I pick for you the best raspberries in our patch. You are so surprised you take them. Encouraged, I learn the Mass at a most precocious age and I am rewarded. I watch you watch my lips, repeating you to you, Kyrie eleison. And I, in my turn, dream. I wish it were me, not you, who was the priest forever, who became God when he served Mass. If I cannot belong to you, I want to be you. If I am you, I am not an outsider. If I am you, I can do for myself what you will not do for me.

So when I take communion from your hands, I imagine I am becoming you who is imagining me. I hold the Host under my tongue until it melts into me, and I become you who dreams of me.

Yet you keep your halo of purity completely intact and inviolate. Resplendent in white on white, you stride across the altar talking confidently to your God: *I have walked in innocence, O Lord, have mercy on me.*

For myself, I pray to the Blessed Virgin: *And after this our exile*.

I study you in the schoolyard. A piece of paper drops from your cassock. I slip inside the gates to pick it up. It has some jottings on it that I can't read and quotation marks around a sentence in block letters: All things betray thee, who betrayest Me.

Dead or alive, it was the same. I wore pink to your funeral. I knew it wasn't the end of us. The newspaper said you had a heart attack. How could that be, one kid cracked, his heart was only a dot. Sister Mary Augusta said that God had called you to Him in your youth. Thirty-five is not youth. I was youth, and you left me.

Right after that, it was summer. The water that year was transparent, dazzlingly light. It was warm. I couldn't stay out of it. The fish were orange and yellow and gold all around me in the blue water. I fell asleep on shore. I dreamed I was swimming in shadow and sand. You were up ahead of me, moving very fast. The wind made your ears blood-red. Your legs were studies in kinetic grace, but so elusive. I couldn't catch you. In my dream, I was small as the moon. I could ride on your back and that made you happy.

For days afterwards, in the worst of the blazing heat, I remembered your back as it felt in the dream, fluid and so cool. And I wondered where you were.

It wasn't all that hard to get to see you. I could summon you by looking at the clown juggling circles on the wastepaper basket in my room. I'd stare at the circles and poke deep into the corners of my eyes. The circles would start to spin until the clown became a golden ball, his nose growing bigger and bigger until it was the chalice with you behind it.

But the chalice caught the sun and the brightness obliterated your face and that wore me out, trying to get past it to see you. It made me mad, and I stopped willing your presence.

Oh, there were questions I would have liked to ask, but they would have gone unanswered in any case. Sin, mostly. I wanted to know the cardinal order of sin. For example, which was worse? Hitting my sister, or not hitting her and hating her? Later on, I wanted clarification on solitary sex. Is there a legitimate use for it, as a last resort, a final defense against the mortal sin of despair? And still later, which is worse, to drink oneself into oblivion or to seek escape through the body of another?

Years passed. When I saw you again, it was as if there hadn't been any years gone at all.

I was a student in Paris, and I met an artist in Montmartre. He was an Englishman. He sat in the open air with his easel and his wine and his small child near him, a daughter, whom he called Fille. The mother had run away from him, he said. I couldn't see why. He was marvelous.

He asked me to gauge the mood of the tourists around me and decide if he should put leaves on the trees he was sketching. "No leaves," I said. "Done," he said, and we went to his little rooms, very close by. I cooked creamed onions according to his instructions. He kept filling up my wineglass. I was too embarrassed to say I had never had more than a sip of wine. Pretty soon my head started spinning, and he said, "I can help you with that. Lie down on the bed and hang your arm over the side." I did. The sheets were coarse and heavy as rugs.

Fille came over and picked my hand off the floor and pushed down on the inside of my fingertips, one by one. "Sing, Fille," said the Englishman. She opened her mouth. She sang: "Souviens-toi de Jésus Christ, ressuscité d'entre les morts. Il est notre salut, notre gloire éternelle." She began again. It was a true and pretty voice, like a bird on a treetop, and I must have dozed off because you appeared before me—barefoot, washing your hands at the side of the altar. I gripped the starched edge of the altar cloth and hung on. You disappeared.

Then it was the seventies, time for politics. My button said, "I am a grass root." The candidate asked me for my help. He believed I could help. I was an ex-housewife. I was nothing, and he asked me to help root out poverty, war and injustice. He said he didn't believe these things had to exist and that none of us could be content until we were all made whole. We heaped our dreams upon his shoulders. And he carried them, carried us, without effort. Later, he weakened.

It was a frantic, febrile time—little sleep, much wine

and so much to do for the candidate. We were lit by a common purpose, and the purpose was to have a common purpose and wipe away particular pasts and failures by doing away with Evil. We lived in a world removed from temporal order. We were all together a single collective mind and body, the mystical body of the candidate.

Stop that talk.

That's what it felt like. We were so many workers among workers and so precise—making plans around the candidate's plans, taking messages, booking travel reservations, typing up the next day's schedule and easing it under the doors of the press, asleep in their hotel rooms, or not.

I did wake-up calls: Good morning Mr. New York Times, it's six-thirty. The press bus leaves at seven forty-five. Coffee and Danish on the bus. Baggage call outside your door in twenty minutes. Good morning, Mr. AP . . . In the beginning, there was always a medium-ripe banana for the candidate's corn flakes. I could set up a press suite at a moment's notice: twelve typewriters, eight phones, a Xerox machine, one telecopier, enough Scotch, more Scotch. And I answered questions. Politely at first, then defensively. Why had the candidate's wife made a pro-abortion speech to Catholics? Didn't anybody brief her? Had the candidate really come out for homosexual marriage?

I was in love with one of the sound men. He was a democrat, small *d*. His own blood had been spilled on the carpet of the Chicago Hilton in 1968. And he knew things. He had gone to El Salvador in the Peace Corps.

One day I helped him wire the sound in a ballroom in the Biltmore. It was that middling time past noon when there is a pause, when a slight change in light suddenly brings you deep into the afternoon. We were drinking wine and trailing wires, looking for the outlets, and we ended up parting the same section of drapes. We closed them around us and it was like a tent in there, warm and cozy and fairly dark. And there was the smell of pine needles, though of course there were no pine needles.

The sound man was quiet, but I could make out his face by the glint of his wire rims. Something must have hit him too because we immediately crumpled together in a swoon. I remember thinking that I wanted to get as close to him as possible, and as I neared that perfect state my mind went completely blank. Moments later, in the sweep of the curtain, the heavy red curviness, I saw you swinging the monstrance at me in a blessing. I was rolling on the floor wrapped in the arms of the sound man and if I have ever been happier, you tell me when.

Go on.

After that, I half expected to open a closet door and find you waiting. (It was a commonplace of the campaign to find unusual activity in closets.) But it turned out to be drink and not a closet that announced you.

I became accustomed to you, to the point of need. You and me and wine in the morning. I knew you were overstepping logical bounds, but I didn't think it strange. To say we knew each other personally, more and more personally, long after you had died was something out of the movies or an asylum. But it was one of those things I just carried in my mind and never thought about.

There came a point—don't ask me when—when the balance shifted. You began to shrink, your shoulders lost their oomph and you seemed more and more distracted, unsure of yourself. I began to pity you, imagining you would have liked to be doing what I was doing, seeing what I saw and having my memories as your own. Getting your fair share, as the candidate was fond of promising each and every American. You who so early on were composed more of a past than a future. I still thought of myself as mostly future.

My sound man did lighting too. Maybe you envied him his say-so over light and dark, because you chose that inconclusive time before dawn, when the morning headache is still building, to remind me just how important was your grip on me. I sensed you hovering nearby, and then I heard your footsteps behind me. My heart began to beat loudly, and it occurred to me, in my sodden state, that this is what I had been born for, to wait for you. My heart, I could feel my heart, and it was your footsteps, inside me, coming after me.

You became a more or less constant presence, someone I could talk to, like a conscience. Or was I yours? I didn't know.

One night I dreamed you told me you had Deutschmann's Disease—with complications. You would not open your mouth because you were afraid you smelled inside. You were, in fact, already dead. I carried you back in the plane in my arms. Your mouth was closed, the back of your neck bubbling black boils, cold like ice, but soft. Mom, you asked (in the dream you called me Mom)— Mom, will the bomb kill me?

There were more campaign mistakes and bigger ones. The candidate signed a petition to give Angela Davis bail, even though she had bought the guns that blew a California judge to pieces. He whispered "Kiss my ass" to a heckler at an airport while he had a microphone around his neck. The scheduling got weirder and weirder— Yuma; Tallahassee; Oxford, Mississippi. Samoa next week, some wise guy told me.

By Halloween, there were fewer of us to make plans, but fewer plans were needed. I was playing poker in the press suite. The sound man had already gone away, without a good-bye. I had spent the afternoon calling everywhere I could think of, but he had vanished, as if there was never anything special between us. I remembered it was supposed to be like that. It wasn't as if we were Weathermen, out to smash monogamy. It was more like, What was the logic of monogamy with so many of us, so many fine, fungible bodies? He had explained that to me. Now, deep in Sunday thoughts, I put down my cards, and my home was exposed: Mother, mentor, lover? There was no one there. I was glad I still had you and I always knew where to find you.

Things began to end badly, in confusion and shame. I'd fall asleep and wake up with my riding boots on and no ideas about why. I'd pace up and down the street across from my apartment in my Earth shoes, reviewing how I had come to this point of pacing. Then it would be the decent hour to buy supplies, and I'd go around the corner, haranguing you about how much wine you made me drink before you let me sleep. I didn't think much about this routine. Everyone in the streets of New York had someone to talk to. Nobody ever said "Be quiet" to us, or "That's enough." We could have gone on for a very long time.

Then one day, or one night, about three in the morning, the sound man called. In those days I interpreted everything that happened—phone calls, the word "hello," rain—as an emergency. This time I had the feeling we were at opposite ends of a long tunnel. He just drew in his breath and I flew with it, and before nightfall I was in California and we were headed to Jackson State Forest. It was a long drive and we drank white wine. On the way, we found some blackberry bushes. We picked so many berries that our hands were stained a deep purple.

We hiked around the mountain. I kept asking to stop and drink wine and make love but he was more interested in hiking. He showed me the sword ferns. We strung a hammock by a stream and we made love in the hammock.

We climbed to a smooth patch overlooking the valley. As soon as we lay down, I wanted to make love. It was around the time of the big trouble at the Three Mile Island nuclear plant. Spring, maybe 1979. He told me about the newspaper reports. I hadn't been keeping up. The farmers of Middletown were quoted on their animals' reactions to the accident. They said their cows "knew" the bubble was melting their babies inside. They predicted that there would be some calves with one ear, others with no eyes, no sex.

It began to get dark. I wasn't distracted by the stories. All I wanted to do was get into my campmate's sleeping bag and rub socks. He was very cross about that. He reminded me of all the times we had made love in the past fourteen hours and he said he was tired of it and that he missed the airline stewardess he really loved. He showed me her picture. It had been taken during the campaign. She was dancing with a reporter. She looked like a child who had been required to learn dancing in school, angular and committed to survival. He said she was an addict now and that she lived alone in Barlow Hollow.

Then he added, gratuitously, I thought, that he hated "my kind." I was the kind of person who wrote letters on airline stationery. I had done that once too often, raising his hopes that an envelope with the return address "The Bluest Skies" was a message from his stewardess. He wished that we were all back starting the campaign again. He for one would have done a better job. At least he would have picked the right people to carry his equipment. There was a lot more hope for society in those days.

I started to get kind of wild in my head and so I got up and began pacing around but it was dark and the fire was nearly out and I was unsteady. I dragged my sleeping bag to the other side of the fire, where by chance I found some more wine. In the embers, I made out your hands fumbling in your cassock for the note you had dropped. I reminded you of what it said, adding that it was from "The Hound of Heaven" by Francis Thompson. You thanked me and we fell asleep together away from the sound man's snore.

You would have liked to have been innocent, but you weren't ever. In your memory, you never were blameless.

No.

They say women like you choose a punishing religion.

Who is they?

It doesn't matter. In your riding boots. Go get it.

No. . . . I've got it. I only wanted to be part of things. . . . There's not much in here.

It's all right. Finish it off. You'll sleep now.

Will it always be like this?

Like this?

Always?

6

CHOICES

OUT OF CONTROL

In the classic story, a man on the brink spends his last afternoon at the beach, deep in outrageous conversation with a child. At dusk he puts on his robe and makes his way back to the hotel room, which smells of nail polish remover. He sits down on his twin bed, looking at his wife, asleep on hers. Then he shoots himself, and the story ends.

In my case, what happened is this: On a sunny day in November, my estranged husband called from Tucson to tell me I was missing something important. My son was growing up. He was going to learn to play soccer. I better get back if I wanted to be in on it. No, I couldn't live with them, there was a student there now to cook dinner and there wasn't any room. But I could get an efficiency nearby and do office temp work. "I have failed every typing test I've ever taken," I said. "You could practice," he said. "You have nothing else to do." "Daniel could play soccer here in Central Park," I said. He said, "Out of the question, we've already had that discussion. And if you sue me, you'll lose."

"Why?" I said.

"Because you abandoned him."

"No, no. Wait. I didn't abandon him. I abandoned you. You promised you would send him when I got settled."

"That's over now. My life is here with my son."

Daniel got on the phone. "Mom, do you know what trust is?"

"That you believe that the other person will do what he says he will do."

"I don't trust you, Mom. I trust Dad. He doesn't move around like you."

I reached for the wine and knocked the phone over and the line went dead. I refilled my glass.

I am always cold in winter. Winter was coming and there was nothing I could do about it. The radio was on: "Some Days Are Diamonds, Some Days Are Dirt" was the song.

I walked over to the West Side Stables. My favorite horse was booked, so I took a new one. He was too rough for me: I tried to rein him in, but it just made him more bent on having his way, all the way to the far north end of the park. I did make it back to the stable without falling off and I told the groom what I thought of the horse. "If you act out of control, your horse is going to pick it up. You lost it today. That's all. It'll come back," he said.

In my room the wind was coming right through the windows. I started back in on the wine, but I could tell it wasn't going to be enough because of the echo in my head: out of control, out of control, out of control. So I fished around and found what I needed: Percodan, Seconal, Stelazine, more than enough. And I took them all and then I waited. Nothing happened. I drank some more, sitting on the floor, knocking my knees against one another. The sound of my knees banging together got louder, finally louder than the noise in my head, and I started to talk to my knees, ugly things, and I started to pick them apart with my hands and I kept going and then I saw something shiny like the inside of an oyster shell. It was the bone. I didn't feel a thing by then and so I opened the window and said, I've found the bones, to the wind and the cold, I've found the bones. It seemed then that only cowards tried to take their lives with wine and pills, and so I yelled, I am a coward, to the cold and the wind. When there was no answer I started to hit things, my typewriter, the table. I beat up my lamp and the whole place went dark.

CHRISTMAS

□

I'm over here in the rocking chair. Don't disturb me. I'll tell you what I'm going to tell you. And that's all.

I just got back from the inkblot test—shoes, burning buildings, ice-cream cones. The last paper he held up was blank. He asked me, so I told him: It reminded me of Mallarmé. Part of a letter, maybe, he sent to a friend, or maybe a line in a poem he wrote when he nearly couldn't write any more. Something like: *L'être est une tache sur la perfection du néant*. Something like: Being is a blot on the perfection of nothingness.

I must really have wowed that doctor.

This woman next to me, adjusting her scarf around her collarbones, is Lillian. She is seventy-eight years old. She says she has learned a lot here, enough to make her better for the rest of her life. No more worrying. Worrying is how she lost forty-three pounds in three weeks.

Tonight Sharon gave Lillian a holy card, a picture of Jesus with long hair and a ring of thorns around His heart. On the back of the card Sharon wrote: "Dear Lillian, May He always be with you."

Lillian started crying because her eyes are brown and His are blue.

But don't let Lillian's girlishness fool you. She knows

things. "Sin cannot love sin" is one of the things she knows.

From my room, the fast, dark river looks cold and wet. But it seems like a childish cold, a childish wet—small, easily overcome from my position here at night, high on a high bed, swaddled in soft white blanketing, heat steaming all around me. In this blur of hot contentment, the boats are playthings, like the little toy boats on the pond at the Tuileries. And way down below, that small form in a pea jacket turned toward the river could be Daniel. And closely next to him, his tall, innocent father.

Apparently, I was asleep in the bathtub when the hotel bouncer broke down the door. "How could she do this to me?" is what Paul said when the hospital called him to check on insurance.

I thought I could actually expunge Patrick if I told Paul about him. So I did, one afternoon after we got our seats in the Tuileries and Daniel was sailing his boat in the shallow waters. We looked like an exceptionally fine family, I thought, a neat, tight little unit. I had just had my eyebrows shaped and I had ironed Paul's work shirt and Daniel had on his navy-blue shorts. He pointed prettily to the other boats in the pond. I took a picture of Daniel pointing to the boats and Paul watching him and then I told Paul I was happy to be out of the desert and I told him why: "Your brother and I had an affair, beginning in the desert and lasting until three hours before the plane took off for Paris. I told your father about it and tried to get him to help me put this family back together again. It was the week you were away teaching the Family Medicine for Poor People seminar at Tufts. He drank for days afterwards, and he kept trying to pull me down in bed with him. We are never going to see your father again."

"How are you going to prove this?"

"What?" I said.

"About my father," he said.

Daniel turned around and came back and Paul held out his arms and Daniel settled in and they hugged. I looked at them through the camera lens. There was no room between them, and the bright light of the sun grew solid around them as they came into focus. It was like watching glue harden. Nothing happens, but you know something is happening.

Even now I have this funny feeling of power about that moment. I had lost them, definitively lost them, but I had, by my betrayal, ensured their future as a couple. Before, the three of us had had this kind of footless, floating, chance togetherness, and suddenly the chanciness had been replaced by something more. The two of them had fused. Though I was no longer with them, it was my sin, my separateness that had permanently bonded them. I had done this myself, against myself, though probably not out of such a generously self-destructive motive. As my friend Kate said later: "Why did you tell him? Were you trying to kill him?"

Oh, but they were beautiful together, and at that moment my heart was filled with love for them. I put the camera back in its cover and snapped the buttons shut. And I thought, I must cook something very good for dinner.

Here at River Bend, we are asked to make common cause with one another. Only the staff, the nurses and the guards and the interns may move about one at a time. When we wait in a clump for the nurse to open the door, she jangles her keys and smiles at us.

And yet, security is loose. Sol was missing for a whole day. He came back in time for dinner with a policeman on either side of him. He showed us how he sprung the lock by running his Visa card through a crack in the doorway.

We must line up if we want anything: to go out, personal supplies, to make a phone call. Those who cooperate receive favors and gifts for the asking. Some are always refused, and still they always ask. I cannot bear to look at their faces, and I never get in line.

I am glad for Lillian, lucky to know her. She is teaching me how to get out of here: "Think slowly."

ABSTRACT

□

(Confidential—For Professional Use Only)

Patient: O'ROURKE, Mary Cecilia, née CRONSTEIN
                328 Riverside Drive
                New York, New York
Admitted: November 17, 1973
Age: 28 (Born February 2, 1946)
Civil Status: Married (Separated)
Occupation: None
Religion: Not Known

CONDITION ON ADMISSION: Stupor. Lethargy. Somnolence. Slow speech. Possible intoxication.

CHIEF COMPLAINT: "I'm sorry it didn't work," in reference to suicide attempt of 50 sleeping pills taken 3 days prior to admission.

PRESENT ILLNESS: About one and a half weeks prior to her overdose she recalled speaking with her husband on the phone but she was cut off. One week prior to her overdose, her son told her that he could not rely on her. Four days prior to the overdose, the patient lost control of a rental horse in Central Park. Two days prior to her overdose, the patient called up her father and canceled a meeting with him. On day of overdose, Wednesday, she postponed a date with her boyfriend, locked the door to her hotel-apartment room, took an overdose of sleeping pills, which she had been gradually taking from his shaving kit for the past six months. She recalls thinking it would be enough to kill her and opening the windows and the phone ringing. She does not recall hallucinations nor removing her clothes as described by friends who found her the following Friday afternoon. She was then referred to River Bend Hospital Clinic.

FAMILY HISTORY: Father is 67 years old, of Jewish background. He is healthy, a retired president of a large company living in San Diego and is described as "totally surprised by everything." Mother is 61, an alcoholic, who lives by herself in Glenview, Connecticut, works in insurance, and is a Catholic. Younger sister, Martha, 24, has been in analysis for two years and is in graduate school at the University of Central Arizona.

PHYSICAL EXAMINATION: Blood Pressure 96/70, Pulse 80, Respiration 16, Temperature 36.6. On admission, patient was still in a semicomatose state. She had friction-type burns on medial aspects of both knees and also flame-type burns on the medial aspects of some fingers. Plastic surgery was done. Treatment was for both knees. Psychological exam revealed her to be out of touch with her feelings while appearing otherwise, with the ever-present danger of impulsively ending her own life. The impression was hysterical personality with depressive features.

AFFECT: She initially appeared drowsy and depressed with negativistic thinking but cooperative, and after sleeping, she seemed like a little girl who had enjoyed doing something wrong. Initially she described herself as hopeless, but the next day reported neutral feelings. She tried to give the impression of contentedness with smiles that seemed uneasy and inappropriate. Although her ideas flowed logically, the content seemed idiosyncratic in terms of what the suicide attempt was about and what she was doing in reference to an apartment, a job and her marriage. Although quite aware of recent events and their meaning, this seemed mostly at an intellectual level and she has used apparently poor judgment in problem solving.

COURSE IN CLINIC: (November 17, 1973, to February 18, 1974)—Patient initially seemed quite intact and capable of masking anger, and manipulating to extricate herself from the hospital. When she became aware that her resistance to treatment could result in mandatory long-term confinement, her formerly strong, organized front seemed to slowly crumble. She became uncertain, depressed, paranoid, and confused over her past behavior. Of note was a long history of suicide attempts beginning in a romanticized way early in life. She was put on thioridazine 200 mg. a day for impulsiveness and anxiety and sleep difficulty, iron for her anemia and one week prior to discharge she was put on Elavil 200 mg. a day for an increase in her depression.

DATE OF DISCHARGE: February 18, 1974

DIAGNOSIS: Depressive Neurosis

STATISTICAL CLASSIFICATION: Depressive Neurosis 300.4

CONDITION ON DISCHARGE: Moderately improved

PROGNOSIS: Fair

A LITTLE LIPSTICK

□

Stooped and dragging, so he notices, I enter the doctor's unremarkable room. One light bulb, about 100 watts, in the corner.

"So." He slaps his knee. "What do you want to do today?"

"I want to jump out the window."

He laughs. "Why?"

"That's all I ever want to do."

"Why?"

"Because my hair is straight, because my son says he can't trust me. Because I can't think of something else to do."

He laughs and laughs. "Such a grand gesture. You like to do the noble thing, don't you? Tell me. How was it in the hospital?"

"Embarrassing."

"You were embarrassed."

"Yes."

"You know, you ought to try putting on a little lipstick. It might make you look pretty. Now, when do you want to see me again?"

Some weeks later, quite casually: "If you think your life is worth so little, give it to me for a year. Then I will give it back, and you can choose again."

95

PRETTY FEET

□□□
□□□

y mother and I had our latest face-to-face in the Glenview train station. I turned thirty-six last month, and it seemed right to visit. Couldn't go forward until I went back? Something like that. I can't say when I first decided to keep away from her because it's only been the last ten years or so that I've actually been able to do it. And it isn't just my mother and I who have grown apart. Some families explode early and never come together. Mine is one of those. We are two daughters and two parents set apart like the corners of a book, each one fixed in place by years of insults and injustices—some real, and some imagined, I was beginning to think.

What I know about my mother and me flows from a

conversation years ago between her and my aunt Fírinn, during which, feeling characteristically sly and powerless, I was hiding behind the couch. I was hoping to hear something that would give me a clue to what was happening in my life. I mean, I really couldn't figure out why God had let my mother and father marry, they hated each other so much, or why I hadn't turned into the boy my father wanted so badly.

My aunt asked my mother how she could have "let it happen again." She was talking about poison ivy. Ever since I first learned to recognize it in the woods, I had given myself the most evil springtime cases of poison ivy, systematically collecting the freshest sprigs, breaking open the stem right below the leaf and rubbing the sap around my eyes and on my ears and throat, and in designs over the rest of my body. I'd be too excited to sleep that night. I'd get up often to stand on the chair next to the sink so I could see myself in the medicine-cabinet mirror. Sometimes it didn't work right away. But it always worked. My face would magically puff out. There would be paths of rose-colored beads, minuscule, but definitely there.

I'd keep going to school until the red paths turned clear, and the glistening beads broke all over, running into a crusty yellow mass that hardened over my eyes and lips and hair. That would be a Thursday, maybe, and I'd stay home from school. Then my mother would come and put cotton dipped in something clear and cool over my eyes.

She'd change the pads often. She'd feed me orange juice, holding the glass for me and parting my lips just a little to let a straw in. I never complained. My father would be concerned. He would say, "How could it have spread that way?" I would ask only one thing, that I hear some music. My parents seemed closer then than at any other time. They talked about me in low voices.

In about two weeks, I would be out of bed, but still so ugly that people gasped when they saw me. A hush stayed over the house for a few more days. And on one of these days, as a special treat, my mother would bring me over to visit my aunt and my cousins. This particular time I heard my mother say something that didn't sink in right away. "Oh, she's fine now. I'm the one. What am I going to do about this rash?" she said, raising her arms high above the sofa. They were, as usual, covered with open sores that looked like insect bites but weren't, because they came all year round.

That was the game for my mother and me. We played victim. Let me tell you, it was hard to win that game. As I grew older, if I had trouble with a boyfriend, she had a husband who not only was Jewish (preventing her from living in Highcliff like my aunt and her Irish husband) but also never came home. If I was sick, she was sick to death. It was so easy to offend her. "I don't know how you could do this to me," she would say. She said it when I married Paul fifteen years ago, a few months after my father moved out of our house. She said it when I told her I was divorcing Paul. She said it when I married Mark. When Mark and I had Addy, I didn't tell her about the baby, but the reproof came anyway. One day out of the blue she called up, wanting to know if what my sister had told her was true. "I don't know how you could . . . " But I had already hung up.

I had become ruthless when it came to a choice between my mother and my children. I first broke with her over my son, Daniel, though I wish to God I had been able to do it sooner. What happened was this: My mother sided with my ex-husband in the divorce. She thought that Paul Noonan O'Rourke, the one who faithfully took her and little Daniel to Mass every Sunday, should raise Daniel. Hers was a formidable opinion, drawing on a great moral force—she was Irish Catholic. She flashed her breeding around as if it were an anointed sword and when she used it on me, it worked. You're right, I said to myself. Why impose my paternal Cronstein legacy on baby Daniel O'Rourke? Why not give him a fresh start? It's the best thing I could do for him. But, of course, it wasn't only that. Maybe I let Daniel go because it made me a winner in our old game. My mother would still have her child, but I wouldn't have mine. In any case, when the divorce came through and Daniel and Paul moved to Tucson, I stopped seeing my mother. But I had weakened a few times lately, inviting her to view Addy in New York. That's when I started having a recurring dream about her and why I finally called up to suggest a visit. I knew she'd be surprised that I wanted to come alone, without Mark, without Addy.

It was a Tuesday morning in early March. Windy and bright at first, then dark as the train got farther away from the station. Big gray-blue mountains of clouds. At Forest Manor, the streetlights were on, and it began to rain. But the sky broke apart again in Wood Haven. A Virgin Mary blue showed through lace clouds, and I relaxed.

My mother, as was her habit, had given me complicated instructions about how we would meet. Untangled, it all meant getting off in Hillbank, where she worked in Herman's insurance office. Herman had hired her one fall day because, she said, "he liked my pretty feet." Herman was nearly blind when he hired her and very sick. My mother nursed him in the hospital and in his home. She tried to bully him into getting better, telling him he was just pretending he couldn't see in dim light, just pretending he couldn't walk when his knees gave way and he fell to the carpet, just pretending he couldn't chew her pot roast with his few teeth. Herman died anyway, and soon, too. My mother went on working in Herman's firm, but she wasn't happy there. Nobody seemed to admire her feet, or anything about her.

I saw her waiting in a small gray car when I walked off the platform. She had wrapped her head in a white turban. Her face was nearly as white, from the baby powder she mixes with her foundation; all that stood out in the marshmallow softness I kissed were her opaque blue eyes. "You're early," she said.

We drove over the bridge and on through another little village before we arrived. I already knew she had sold our old house in Hillbank and moved into a "somewhat smaller" place, but I wasn't prepared for this tiny ground-floor apartment. It was so full of stuff, all things, I realized slowly, she had saved from the basement of the old house. Every surface of the basement furniture was slipcovered with scraps of material from dresses we girls had worn when we were small. The scraps were patched together and collected at the edges with elastic. It looked like the sofas and the chairs and the footstools—there were a lot of footstools—were wearing shower caps.

The clutter was unbelievable. She had sold everything of value, not to start anew, it seemed, but to make room for her mementos and collections. She had saved the bows from poinsettia plants, broken bookends, chipped ash-trays, probably a dozen pair of castanets from her trips to Cuba. She had sold the bone china she bought in England, France and Finland and kept the plastic imitation Wedg-wood my uncle's factory had discontinued before it was ever distributed. Her standup kitchen was hardly even that. The floor, and most of the counter, were taken up with her collections—plastic bags in paper bags, smaller paper bags in a large paper bag, uneven stacks of plastic containers, smoothed-out pieces of aluminum foil and half-gallon jugs of gin.

She opened the icebox to get some milk. It was crammed full of dented cans with no labels and other unrecognizable substances wrapped in plastic bags with rubber bands around them. In the old days, the icebox arrangements at least would have been partially offset by my father's red caviar, his imported kippers, his smoked salmon, his special breads, his rare wines and pricey liqueurs. And the chipped ashtrays would have been out of sight. My father hated broken things. In his rooms, in the old days, he kept his books, his first editions, his turn-of-the-century watercolors, his piano, his original manu-script collection, and his eighteenth-century music box that looked like a coffin on top of four huge, curvy legs.

No question that my mother finally had her way with a home, but really there was nothing charming about this decor. These things all over, in no order of importance, were, nonetheless, all of a piece. Parts of me were there too. It was my broken colored pencils she had saved, my moth-eaten stuffed animals. It hurt to be attached to this tangle and it felt menacing, as if I were suddenly very small again and the whole mess could engulf me.

"Mom, why are you saving these pencils? They're no good anymore."

"I put them out for Addy. It's a shame you didn't bring her. I don't know how—"

"Mom," I overlapped. "I've been having dreams about you. The same one over and over."

"Just a minute, Lovey. I see an ant." She fished a used

paper towel out of the garbage and trapped a bug on the counter. I started talking:

"In my dream I'm running around the reservoir. But my feet keep getting stuck on the ground, and I start slowing down. I know that if I turn around, I'll unlock my legs and spurt ahead. But I don't want to because you're there and you're furious because I've eaten all the icing off the coffee ring. So I don't turn around and I keep going forward, but slower and slower. Of course I never get all the way around. I wake up really tired."

"Are you asking me for some coffee cake?"

"No, I'm telling you my dream."

"Well, it doesn't surprise me. You never could share with your sister." She made a sign with her hand for me to get out of the way so she could get by with the coffee. I followed her into the living room.

"What's this?" I asked, picking up two maid's aprons from bygone days, now covered with pencil marks and straight pins, so I could sit in the chair that looked like my old yellow-flowered dress.

"Oh, don't disturb those. I'm making lamp shades out of them. Sit over here." (On my sister's polka-dot skirt.)

She poured some coffee into the mock Wedgwood cups. I sat mine on the end table next to the dog bookends. One dog was missing a leg but it still held up a book, a leather-bound copy of *Nana*. "Your father gave that to me before we were married, when I took a cruise to Cuba," she said. "I was traveling long before he ever thought of it, you know. I love marine life. If I had had the chances you girls had I would have been a deep-sea diver." Her face settled into a square. "How is your father?"

"Fine, I think." I had no idea.

"Oh."

"How is Paul?" I countered.

"Very well. He'll probably call tonight. He calls every week so I can talk to my grandson. Paul says Daniel wants to stop being an altar boy."

"Sounds right. He's almost fifteen."

"Paul is a very good Catholic."

"A very good Catholic," I agreed.

"You know what I mean. He's pure. He's pure Catholic."

"I know what you mean. Mom, why did you marry somebody Jewish if you hate Jews so much?" (I had never tried that one before.)

"I don't hate anybody. Besides, what does that have to do with you? I spent every minute taking you girls to church and confession and Mass and Sunday school. Is it my fault you didn't live up to the fact you are Catholic? I did my best."

"We all did our best, Mom."

"Do you know there's a law—a Jewish man who marries a Christian and has children, those children are automatically Christian."

"You told me that."

"Well, then."

We sipped our coffee. She blew her nose and pushed her hair back. She's the only blonde and the only one with curly hair in our family.

"I still don't know how you are going to turn out," she began as I was starting to ask her why she liked Paul so much. "I'm sorry, Lovey, what did you say?"

"I was asking you if you remembered the fight you had with Paul when Daniel was just a few days old." She looked blank. "You must remember," I urged. "Paul was walking you back to your motel and you told him that Daniel was crying because my milk wasn't good and Paul turned on you and said, How could you know, had you tried it?" (My mother had been so offended she didn't come over the next day. I went to find her. She was in her motel room with the shades drawn and a glass of gin next to her. She was crying. I coaxed her back to the apartment by promising that Paul would never talk like that again.)

"I don't remember anything of the sort. You must have made that up. Paul has always been a gentleman. I still don't know how you are going to turn out," she said again. Then she said, "Your sister is Jewish now. She converted."

"Why? What did it matter?"

"I don't know why. She's old enough to know better.

But she always tried to please your father. She was terribly hungry for his love, I guess. Of course, she couldn't get it. You had it all."

News to me. I smiled, trying to picture my father and me in a room together. She went on.

"I tried so hard to protect you children. Ever since the Holocaust, I wanted you to be known as Christians, not Jews. Prejudice is a heartache, and it's all over Foxford County."

Once again, you can't move to Highcliff, only now it's a daughter who's the spoiler, I almost said, but didn't. Why turn over old stones? It was as if she heard me anyway. Her face screwed up and she started picking a sore on her leg.

I looked down at her fine hair and wondered what it would have been like to be my aunt's daughter, raised in Highcliff, the town without Jews. My mother had made it seem like Paradise whenever we drove over. She'd point out the beautiful houses there and show us the club we could never join, though she often suggested, in private, that I might get in, maybe as a single member, if I dated boys with the right last name. She never said we couldn't live in a beautiful house in Highcliff. She just pointed them out. Mostly my father pretended not to notice. He's the kind of person who cannot bear unpleasantness unless it's part of an opera. The worse things got, the more he turned up the volume on the radio. Later he traveled. One Thanksgiving, he did shoot back at Mom. We had stopped for a red light right before my aunt's house. He turned off the ignition, poked my mother in her puffy cheek and said: "Pigs eat ham." And he laughed, a long whistle-laugh.

"Open the hamper in the hall," my mother broke in. "I think there are some shoes there that might fit you."

In the hamper, the shoes were paired and put into old cinnamon-colored stockings. I browsed while my mother told me the same old Winkelman story.

"You know I had to have my shoes made for me because my feet were so small. Mr. Winkelman made them himself. But every time one of you girls came along, my feet grew a half size. They were perfect right before you were born—a four and a half. Mr. Winkelman asked me if I would model in his store. I had to say no because I was already pregnant and your father didn't like the idea anyway. Not that he was around much by then."

I looked into the hamper at the shoes, all pumps or strapless, all fancy, all evening. I saw my mother dancing on the deck with my father, the way I had never seen them together, though there was a picture of them somewhere sitting on bar stools when she was young and flowering. The idea seemed plausible. He would be wearing a linen jacket and those fancy spectator sport shoes or maybe even saddle shoes. On the boat he wouldn't have a car. No one would know he drove a Cadillac, maybe one like the one he gave me on my sixteenth birthday, the one I wouldn't drive again after my friend Grace Ann called it a Jew Canoe.

My mother pulled out a pair of walking shoes with a buckle. "Here, these are for you. I bought them while I was carrying you, and then I outgrew them after you were born."

"They're quite nice. And they fit. Thank you," I said.

I kept them on as I paced the platform waiting for the train home. Pretty soon the small toe of each foot hurt, so I went into the comfort station and put Band-Aids on my feet. I threw my own shoes away. I hate carrying anything extra. Going home, I tried to think about nothing.

The train passed Highcliff. "My mother says she raised us Catholic in case there's a Holocaust in Foxford County. Do you believe that?" I asked the window. The window shot back my old nightmare: Daniel and I are in the camp. He is inside me. We are tied to a walnut tree, just as he starts banging out to be born.

I wiped my hand against the window. It came back filthy. "You know," said my daytime self, "you like to exaggerate. That way you don't have to deal with the real thing."

That evening I met Mark at the Salon de Kyoto. He thought we should try something new, so we were having a shiatsu massage. We took off our coats and undressed in a room with shutters, soaps and sprays. All around us were naked bodies shielded by shutters. We were led to the sauna, where we sat a short time and got very hot. A woman gave us ice water in plastic glasses. Then two ladies ushered us into a room with two cots. The light was low—a towel covered the bulb. There was a hole at the upper end of each cot. My lady settled my face in my hole. I looked down, and I could see her feet on the carpet in front of me. They were covered in white cotton slippers with the big toe separated from the other toes. Pretty soon, she hopped on my back and dug her toes in on either side of my spine. The two women whispered a lot to each other in Japanese.

And I lay on my white sheet covered by another white sheet next to my husband in his white sheets. I felt like I was a suburban housewife in from the country to do something hot but sinless, and that I would soon go home and talk about it over coffee with my favorite neighbor in my kitchen. When I turned over, my lady said, "Hurt?" and pulled at the Band-Aids on my pinky toes.

"No. My shoes are too small."

"Pretty feet," she said, picking up one foot and smacking the instep.

INTIMACY

The last time I saw my son, Daniel, he was on the other end of the electronic screener in the Tampa airport. He was on his way back to his father in Tucson and he was happy. He couldn't stop waving. That was three years ago. I'm a believer, and in those days I was a believer in the theory of inherited addiction. The night Daniel came to New York for his scheduled visit, I was at my regular AA meeting in the basement of an old church, and Daniel came to find me there. In AA, we call the church Our Lady of the Wok because the statue of the Virgin looks like it's crowned with a cooking instrument. Daniel thought that was a pretty funny name. Then he asked me what AA was, and I told him, and he said, in his easy sociable way, "Maybe I'm an addict too," and he pulled out his stash of chemicals and weeds. He tried to put it back in his pocket, but it was too late. The next day I whipped him off to Florida, to a little cottage by a stagnant pond that specializes in teenage drug use. It was the mosquito season. Daniel stayed three weeks. They wanted him to make a commitment—to their program, to God and to sobriety. He wouldn't. He kept saying, "My mother made me do this."

I watched Daniel waving at me in the airport. His smile appeared and disappeared as his arm moved across his face, steady as a metronome. "Addicts wave that way," I yelled. "Good-bye, Mom," he said.

And now, he's coming back to go to college. Eberhard College in Connecticut is impressed with his survival skills in the rootless no-school scene, the admissions dean told him, and his initiative. He took the high school equivalency test after freshman year. They don't seem to care that Daniel's main activity is sleeping. Most all the classes happen after six, it says in the catalogue.

Daniel comes in from Tucson in the dead of night. He has a ring in his nose and his hair is about the same length as Farrah Fawcett's. We look exactly alike except for the ring. "Weird," he says. "You are a walking mirror. I can't stand it."

Daniel goes straight to bed. In the morning, Addy looks him over. "Should we make an appointment to have his hair cut?" she asks. Addy is four. She likes to get things done.

"Let's let him wake up first," Mark answers. And he tucks Daniel in a little tighter and arranges his hair over his ears and says to me and Addy, "Come along, my pets."

All of the women in our family are pets. Mark has three grown pet daughters, Veronica, the Brown graduate turned waitress, Caroline, the street musician, and Alison, the accountant. Then there is Addy, half-sister to Veronica, Caroline, Alison and Daniel, and then there is me. We are all interchangeably "my pet," "sweet thing," "angel cake." Most of the time I am "angel cake," though every so often, in the heat of pleasure, I am "Daniel." This is highly disconcerting when it happens.

There are many fused families like ours in the neighborhood and even on the East Side. But my family is the only one I know where the husband is in love with the stepson. Theirs is a bizarre relationship, uncomplicated, I am prepared to believe, by sex. Mark writes the letters that Daniel never answers, goes to the post office before breakfast with packages for Daniel, sends him checks, invites him home, begs him to buy a functional pair of shoes—the way I used to, but don't anymore.

Can a stepfather love a stepson purely and unselfishly in thought, word and deed? The answer to this question is none of my business, say my AA friends. My business is not to drink. If I don't drink and go to meetings everything will be all right. Besides, Mark is my bridge back to

Daniel. I will betray Mark, of course—out of jealousy, out of the routine loneliness of marriage.

But not this year. This is the year I'm supposed to learn how to swim fearlessly so I can teach Addy. Her motor skills are underdeveloped, the testing people say. She will never get into kindergarten if I don't stop buttoning her sweater and tying her sneakers. Instead, I must teach her to do these things on her own and we must swim together and play catch and draw pictures so she can strengthen her "weak crayon grip."

In any case, it's not chic in the late eighties to have affairs. It's chic to exercise and substitute familial intimacy for autoerotic addictions like wine and chocolate. This is the time to value fantasy over experience.

Accordingly, these days I am a woman who plays it safe.

These days, I am a woman whose husband is in love with her son.

Mark is in crisis this year. His dreams of Charles de Gaulle have escalated. Almost every night I am awakened by his voice, tense and excited: "Oui, mon général."

Mark's mission in life is to keep the world under control. It's part of his constant battle against humiliation, humiliation being anything he has not already decided will happen. Organic growth in any form upsets him. Once, while he was away for a week, I replaced a ficus tree with a healthy one twice its size. "What's wrong with that plant," he said, visibly shaken, when he saw it. The unplanned illness, the unplanned tantrum, the unplanned food for dinner, or anyone he can describe as a "loose cannon on the deck"—it's all so hard on him.

To keep control, he practices self-discipline: one half English muffin and coffee in a demitasse cup every morning. He trims excess material possessions. Except for what I hide under the bed—Addy's baby things—there is nothing without an immediate use in our house. Mark's biggest success in efficiency and order is our kitchen equipment. In our kitchen we have three pots, one small, one medium and one large, and we have one frying pan with a glass cover so we can see the state of what is cooking.

At night, with his friends, Mark plots campaigns to control the world. When I first met him, I assisted at long evenings at P. J. Clarke's when the topic was how one was going to get into Hubert Humphrey's cabinet. Now they are into Institutes. They have noticed that the new tax law penalizes corporations that don't give away money. Next year, Mark's crowd reasons, there will be a flood of money available for worthy institutes. One will start an institute where important people will assemble to discuss the world and how it should be. It will be in a townhouse and there will be many servants and many black-tie dinners. One hopes it will be a good year for Beaujolais. It all works very well for Mark at night. But, come morning, it's a different, sad story. Generals do not take the subway to work.

I can tell when Mark is thinking about the subway. He'll be on his way out the door. He'll offer his cheek, soft and sweet from a recently applied cocoa butter stick. Then, remembering something from the middle of the night (probably my frail but frequent request, "Let's let fate choose if there'll be a baby or not"), he'll say (to the closet) that for my own good there will be no more pets and that it is futile to wish for more or even for a new husband. "No one will ever love you better than me."

This last is profoundly distressing to me although I suspect he's right. However, one can live for the moment, can't one? My old lover, Joe, the Haight-Ashbury dope dealer, showed me how to do that, and it's kind of a habit with me now. He was a beautiful stranger, came late and stayed the night. The only day we spent together was when we drove up the mountain where Wavy Gravy's ladyfriend was about to give birth. Joe's pain-relieving expertise was needed. As it turned out, the happening didn't happen, but neither one of us ever got over the idea of him as a midwife. With the change in times, he became a retailer of "natural" things from Hong Kong. He spoke eloquently about his business—praising the endurance, steadfastness and loyalty of a certain all-cotton nightshirt, the particularly fluffy filaments inside his imperial down comforters and pillows. He married and divorced often and I couldn't tell one wife from the other from the way he described them (so different from his comforters). Except when a child was born and he was midwife to his wife. Then, on the telephone, he reenacted the scene for me, so vividly I could feel him—burrowing deep into the terror of the hour, crooning and wiping and soothing, until finally, his moment came, and he held the slippery baby up, fixed it firm in his stranger's grasp.

He calls now and then, and every time I get caught up in the grasp of his voice, and I start thinking about those babies coming into his hands. I picture myself in California on the natural-fiber fabric bed in his yellow house, surrounded by the children and the wife and the ex-wives and flowers and ferns and ficus trees. It's my turn with my new baby and he comes to me, and I sweat and scream and bite my pillow. The branches in my neck harden and stand out and rail against the insult of separation. And then I push and he pulls and there she is, one moment in his hands, the next on my breast. Joe is already gone by then, but it's a long time before I notice.

His name isn't really Joe. It's David. Joe is what Mark calls him from a line in "The Stranger Song": "He was just some Joseph looking for a manger." Now I call him Joe too.

□

We drive Daniel to Connecticut to Eberhard. After registration, during which he tells the school nurse that he has had bouts of anxiety, depression and nervousness and has been treated for drug addiction, he puts his head in his pillow and says he needs a nap. We leave the room and walk through glens and close to forests. We sit down in the shade under a willow tree. I am reading about Andrew Wyeth's secret mistress, hoping it is not a hoax. Mark is mapping out an essay about the state of the world: "We live in an age of doctrines, where ideology is not always adhered to but where it is, surely, sorely needed. It represents . . . " Addy draws a picture of a girl who has lost her tooth. The girl gets presents when she loses her tooth—a new house, a lot of hair, and a male sex organ.

"Why these presents?"

"Then I'll have everything."

"Won't you be lonely having everything all by yourself?"

"Why?"

By and by we see two boys on bikes in the distance. One of them has hair like Daniel's but it's too early in the day for Daniel. I go on reading. The boys come closer, careening toward us down the hill, no hands. One of them is Daniel. He is laughing and his arms are outstretched: "Shall we separate the rose from the darkness," he shouts, flying past us. My son, the sleep addict, is a live boy on a bicycle, in daylight, in summer. I dig an X in the earth to mark Eberhard's first miracle.

Daniel is three weeks into school. It is still August. The school has an ungraded initiation period. Everyone reads and writes and gives performances. Daniel has given several performances. One was a reading of his poem in the manner of J. Alfred Prufrock. He reads the poem to me over the phone. It is more words than I have heard from him in a whole year. Daniel says he loves school. He loves it because it is so beautiful, because the sky reminds him of the state of Idaho, where his girlfriend, Cynthia, is.

We visit him and he shows us his room. It has a mattress on the floor and the desk and dresser in front of the mattress, "so I can get a little privacy." On his bulletin board, there is a picture of Cynthia in a green wash showing only her eyelashes clearly, very full eyelashes, and Addy's drawing of herself with her missing tooth and her presents.

We go out to lunch and stop in the hardware store. Daniel chooses an electric-coil water heater, black cups for tea, and two cranberry candles in little holders that look like glass flower pots. He thinks a hamper and a floor lamp would make his "space" look more like home, "more intimate." How about a few books, I almost say, but keep my little joke to myself.

Mark writes a note to Daniel telling him how wonderful it was to be walking with him at Eberhard near the big fir trees and under the scuttling clouds. And "Did I ever tell you how much I love your laugh?" Really.

Addy and I both have our mind on babies. I tell her she will have to have them for me. She says she and William, the super's son, will have twins. She dictates a note to William: "Dear William, I love you. We'll have so much fun dancing and I can't wait to have our babies." She takes the elevator to the basement to deliver her letter and comes back with William.

Addy and William dress for their wedding—jewels, necklaces, clips and bows in their hair. William can't find the right clothes to wear, so he stays in socks and no clothes, packing to go away. They are going to Australia by canoe. The canoe is made with sofa pillows and lined with stuffed animals. They get in. Addy plays "Over the Rainbow" on her wind-up music pillow.

It's vacation time. Mark takes Addy off to Little Basin, Rhode Island, to his ancestral ground, where he still has all his tricycle friends. It's his time alone with Addy. It's my time to learn to scuba dive. Mark says, "Don't swim too far; no one will ever love you better than me." He hands Addy her backpack full of rag dolls: "Come, my pet," he says.

"You must have me mixed up with someone else," she says, strapping her children onto her back.

I head for Key West, where I will swim all day and go to meetings at night. That way I will stay out of trouble where, I hear, it is easy to get into trouble—the night breeze is just too soft.

My scuba instructor is a hefty sort, name of Marlene— gentle, all-knowing, serious. We get down to business under the umbrella by the swimming pool. I take apart my breathing device, called a regulator. I examine it closely, spit into it, put it back together and bite down on the mouthpiece. I'm ready. I put on my weights and swagger to the edge of the pool. I take a giant stride off the deep end. I deflate my life jacket and sink. At the bottom of the pool, slumped over, is Barbara, the ex-marine with blue eyes. She draws her index finger across her throat, signaling she is out of air. I am to rescue her. My mask fogs up. I take my regulator out of my mouth, put it in hers. She breathes once, twice. I am blowing bubbles and waiting. Marlene is hovering over me, watching. I breathe two long breaths. We pass the breathing device back and forth and swim to the shallow end, sharing our air. I love rescue. Marlene says I took three breaths all the way down. "That's not sharing," she says, sternly.

In the evening I sit, waterlogged and strong, at meetings. The children of alcoholics meet. The alcoholics meet. The friends of alcoholics meet. Addicts Anonymous meets. I am the only mother of an addict who is also an addict at the meeting for the friends of addicts.

At a meeting, I am asked to tell my story. I tell the story of a woman drinking alone, ordering wine from different liquor stores, so as not to draw attention that a case of wine is being delivered to a one-room apartment every other day. I tell them about a mother waking up and looking over at the boy beside her, seeing burn marks on his arm, and asking, "What happened to you?" And about the boy who sleepily replies, "Oh, you remember, your cigarettes, when we were playing spit."

"I never play cards with a cigarette in my hand. I'm too slow if I do."

"It's all right, Mom, you said you were sorry."

At night I study my Open Water Sport Diver manual and practice in my Open Water Sport Diver workbook. It's grim stuff: List four symptoms that indicate a diver may have an air embolism: bloody froth at the mouth and nose; blindness; deafness; paralysis. . . . The coral that can give you slow-healing sores when you touch it is (fire) coral. Stingrays are difficult to see because they (bury) themselves in the ocean floor.

It's a lot like the Baltimore catechism on sin actually. (Lapsed Catholics often have a good memory of the Baltimore catechism, especially for the questions about sin.) For example, actual sin. Haven't thought of it in years but I know that "Actual sin is any willful thought, word,

desire, omission or action forbidden by the law of God."
And then of course, mortal sin. Mortal sin is a grievous
offense. It "takes away the life of the soul and condemns
the sinner to the everlasting fires of hell." Then there are
the conditions that must be present to make a sin mortal:
"To make a sin mortal these three things are necessary.
First, the thought, desire, word, action or omission must
be seriously wrong or considered seriously wrong; second, the sinner must know it is seriously wrong; third,
the sinner must fully consent to it."

I fall asleep with sin on my mind but hope in my heart.
What a gift.

In the van on the way to my first ocean dive, Marlene
and I eat wheat-flour Fig Newtons and drink canned iced
tea. At the dock, I lug the air tanks onto the boat. We
shove off with about forty other sport divers. It's a little
choppy, a little mean-looking. Too late I realize I'm much
more suited to diving in a swimming pool. There's so
much water out here. The boat stops. Two by two the
divers descend. I sit next to my buddy Marlene on the
ledge of the boat. She pushes off. It's my turn. I'm still
sitting and peering into the water. "Go," I hear. "Go," I
hear again. Then, from far away, "No one will ever love
you better than me."

And I push off, breathing hard, sucking in oxygen for
all I am worth. I surface briefly and plunge down, past the
giant pink pulsing jellyfish, down to the reef, marker
number one, home of a million beautiful things, Marlene

has told me, and she's right. Standing at the bottom of the ocean, I give the okay sign to Marlene, though one ear is killing me. She gives me the sign to "equalize." I hold my nose and blow—gently, harder, gently, harder. At last, it really is okay. We do the exercises for my test. I take off my mask, put it back on, and clear it, and clear it again, and again. It's still half full of water. Clear it again. We swim around sharing my air, looking into each other's eyes for signs of distress. Her eyes are enormous. I navigate with my compass—out 180 degrees for twenty-five kicks, back 180 degrees for twenty-five kicks toward Marlene's okay sign. The sign means that I have conquered the underworld. I feel like Alexander the Great, but I also feel kind of light-headed. Fool around, Marlene motions, and I follow her at a discreet distance.

I am at the bottom of the ocean swimming among the innocent. Addy and Daniel are with me. They flow in and out of my ears like a whisper, like slow breathing. They are safe in me. I am that fish who swallows her young and harbors them within until they are grown big enough to fend for themselves. We three are one within one in the place where it all began. At last. What was the point of evolution, anyway?

Marlene stops and pulls a knife from inside her right calf. She cuts a sea urchin off the coral, opens it and feeds the fish. I have trouble achieving "neutral buoyancy"— my feet are either dragging the sand or I am up too high.

The fish on their reef go about their lives with the

assurance of priests on the altar. Trying to stay in one place, I kneel and dig my fins into the sand. I feel them sink deep into the torn leather of the altar-rail cushions. I am seven years old, wearing stiff white organdy that stings the back of my knees. The puffy sleeves scratch my arms, and the bobby pins holding my veil stick into my scalp. In the warm, clear water the fish go by me, scores of virgins without number "terrible as an army with banners," I bubble out, beautiful in their holiness of purpose, their stately, sure, swift majesty.

I rise, my feet burning, my knees raw, and I follow a school of yellowtail to the mouth of the coral. Marlene pokes me and shows me that my air supply is in the red zone. She points up. When we surface, she looks me over. My knees and ankles are covered with scratches. "Fire coral," she says. "You should watch where you are going and you should watch out for the plants. You have to respect them. It's hard for them to grow down there. You are the biggest fish in the water and you can do some harm." Really.

In my meetings, I am busy. I make coffee for the seven o'clock group. The water has a slimy look. I pour it out. It still has a slimy look. I cannot serve the coffee I make. "One day you will wake up, and you will feel that a weight has been taken from you. You will understand that you will never forgive yourself, but you will also realize that you are strong enough to live with yourself. This is called grace. It always happens," says the man whose daughter jumped off a cliff in Topanga Canyon. He makes fresh coffee for me. It's very good.

I take the plane north to Little Basin. I wear high, high heels and a short skirt and my sports injuries. I am tan and healthy and my hair is curly and Mark is impressed and Addy shows me how she can dive into the waves too. We go back to New York in triumph.

There is a letter from the draft board for Daniel. Their computer has matched his birth date with a list provided by the Motor Vehicle Bureau. He is past the age when he must register for the draft. "Sign here that you intend to register." There is no warning of penalty. I forward the letter together with an offer of a free Uncle Sam T-shirt if the draft-age boy accepts free information on Army opportunities, understanding that he is under no obligation.

Daniel says registration would be a complicitous act, that it would put him in the system of "imperialist democracy." What? "There is no place we are defending that we haven't already taken from somebody else," he explains.

Reason and logic fail me. I say nothing and just hope the draft doesn't catch up with him before the semester is over, in case he actually finishes a whole semester. Daniel wants to talk to Mark. Mark stays hunched over the receiver until dinner is ready. He's so involved he doesn't notice I let the pasta overcook, overcook meaning past the point he likes it. "What did Daniel want?" I ask.

"Oh, nothing, the meaning of life, ennui, sex, not much. I think he's ready for Rimbaud. I'll get it for him tomorrow." Mark searches out his copy and leafs through it. "You know," he says, "Rimbaud was the seducer. Verlaine was ten years older than Rimbaud, but Rimbaud seduced him." Later, I think. Later I will deal with this. If Daniel will just stay put for a few more weeks, I will deal with it then.

We are writing out applications for Addy for kindergarten. The school wants to know what qualities make her a good candidate for kindergarten. It is raining. It is cold. We are at the computer. I am sitting on a stool beside Mark dictating Addy's attributes, her strengths and weaknesses: She can count to a hundred. She loves the waves. She loves her brother, Daniel. She can tie her shoes if she is in a good mood. She thinks she can read.

"Do you want me to help you or not? Stop fooling around," Mark says.

The phone rings. It's my old lover. He'll be in New York in an hour and a half. "For goodness' sake, why don't you call me tomorrow?"

"When can I call? Eight? Nine? Ten?"

"Okay," I say. My knees are weak but I needn't have bothered to feel bothered because Mark says:

"Who was that?"

"My old lover."

"Good old Joe. He never loved you. I am your life."

"Do we need to tell these schools that Addy sucks her thumb?" I ask.

I borrow my best friend's red sweater and I get up early next day to wash my hair. Joe calls. I walk across the park to his address, the ground-floor apartment of a friend of his. He's dressing when he opens the door. I resist the urge to button his shirt.

Joe is here to meet with the Feather and Down Association and representatives of the U.S. Government. They are preparing for high-level trade talks with the Chinese. Duck down is a strategic war material and the Pentagon has been frustrated in its efforts to secure a steady supply. Joe's negotiating techniques ("sit very still and look perplexed") have made him a big success with the Chinese and now everyone wants to know how he does it. Joe has a lot of meetings today. The phone rings and rings. There is not much time.

We sit. He makes tea, herbal tea. He tells me about his life, "just a continuation, really." There is the latest baby. Show me your hands, I say. He does. They look ordinary. I give them back and ask if he can tell I'm different—"I'm a certified scuba diver."

"Oh, yeah? Did you see Jesus down there?"

"How did you know?"

"Everybody does."

Then he talks about his diving, that he's not certified but he's been "down very deep" with a friend who took him looking for sharks. He found sharks. He faced sharks. He even stood on a shark. I give up.

Is there no way out of this briar patch, no way back to that brief meadow of a time when I got messages like "Just calling" or "I missed my plane but it was worth it"—no way at all?

I tell him about the baby we almost had but I decided not to have. I blow my nose a lot, but that's because I have a cold. He is calm except for a slight quiver in the cheek. I don't reach for him and he doesn't reach for me. We look out the window.

I hear from deep inside me, "Say you wouldn't do it again. Not for anything." I say nothing. Joe's taxi arrives.

I pick up Addy from school. We find William and go to the park. They start with the swings. On the theory that you have to exercise the brain or it dies, I pull out my scuba-diving workbook. But the mind rebels: "Why did God make me?" it asks. And it answers: "God made me to know, love and serve Him in this world and to be happy with Him in the next." Taking my mind in hand, I search the workbook for a dive problem. I find one: "A buddy team dives to 85 feet for 15 minutes. After the dive, they rest on the surface for 65 minutes and then descend to 55 feet for 30 minutes to find artifacts. Plot their repetitive groups including what group they will end in, residual nitrogen times, and bottom times on the accompanying dive profile."

Inside the oval fence in this, Addy's favorite, playground, there is a huge tree with yellow leaves. In the Indian summer November dusk, the leaves have a great, fruitlike weight. Addy gathers them by the armful. She is making a sculpture. It's a volcano, she says, scooping up the leaves and tossing them into the air again and again.

9

BLOWS

When the blows started coming I thought, It's just like the saying says, they fall like rain. Like rain falling on the slate terrace of the old house, a hard insistent rain, drops so big and wide, splattering, and me watching them from my bedroom window. He had me pinned on the pillows, the covers were down. It was a hot night, but I felt cold as stone, marked and cooled by the rain. I could feel where he was above me, naked like me, but loud, loud in the black night, pounding on one shoulder, on my good arm where all my strength is. *My husband beats his wife*, I thought then, and just as I thought it, he turned on the light and I raised a hand like a stop sign and he grabbed my hand and trapped it with his knee.

I looked up into his small cellular face and then at his neck, pale as a root, where his sleep mask was hanging, the smooth cords black on his neck and chest, the skin gone soft, soft under the white hair of his chest. I saw his ragsoft skin. And I thought, If I stay limp, maybe he will stop, and then I noticed that the door was open and I cursed the open door and the mindless noise of his voice that filled the room and spilled out into the corridor. And I was ashamed of him going on and on and me just lying there, and I prayed to make him stop before we got into Addy's dreams. They say children hear noise like that, hear it in their sleep and remember it all their lives, remember it as some faraway thing, a faraway cry that urges them to get up and go away to a quiet place. And I knew then it was my own mother's crying that was coming through the pouring rain that night I climbed out of my bedroom window onto the deeply slanted roof and inched my way on all fours to the edge where the gutters were stopped up from the oak leaves. And when I had thrown the oak leaves out onto the terrace, splat, splat, splat, and the water poured down free and clear, I inched back up to where the outside attic was, the one with the door on the deeply slanted roof that no one was supposed to open. And I knew no one would follow me there, and so I opened the door and crawled inside where it was dry and small like a pocket.

But the hitting wasn't about gutters or oak leaves or pockets or even rain on the terrace of the windy dark house. It was nothing personal at all, he said while inspecting my shoulder. He told me: "I am a speeding train and I am knocking you out of the way. You could be anyone."

HEARTWORLD

LEARNING TO READ

The day after Mark left, I said to Addy, "Let's eat out tonight." She was surprised—I guess she could smell dinner already cooking—but she didn't hesitate, just started heading for the door. It was such a warm evening there was no need for jackets. So we were all set. I turned off the oven. The potatoes were almost done, too hot to handle. I left them in. On the way out, I folded back the tablecloth over my new pamphlets—"The Battered Wife Syndrome" and "Step-by-Step to Self-Esteem." There wasn't anyone around to see that they were there, but I felt better after I covered them up.

I couldn't remember when just the two of us had been

out to dinner together, except to McDonald's when we were on the highway. Mark hates that food, so he always waited in the car. This will be good, I thought. We won't have to hurry.

"Let's go to the café," I said.

"What?"

"Come on. I'll show you."

Around the corner, up one block and across the street, there is a restaurant with tables outside. It looks out on the dry cleaner's. I remembered Mark had some shirts there I hadn't picked up yet and I made a mental note to get them, but not tonight.

Addy wanted a table with an umbrella. That was easy. All the tables had umbrellas. The waiter handed her a menu. She opened it up immediately and picked up the edge of the paper that was stapled to the menu covers.

"What does this say?" she asked.

"Specials for the Week. It means that each day of the week the cook makes something he's especially good at for dinner. What would you like to eat now?"

"Just a minute. What day is today?"

"Thursday. Would you like some french fries?"

"Okay."

So I asked for that and a bowl of onion soup and two green salads. I said we'd wait and see about a main course. The waiter asked if the young lady would like a Coke. "She doesn't drink Coke," I said.

"I'd love a Coke," said Addy to the waiter.

The waiter took away the menus but Addy wanted hers back. "You ask, I'm too shy," she said. The waiter gave back her menu. She stood it up on the table and put her head in between the covers.

A peaceful evening, I thought, and folded my hands in my lap. There was a guy walking up and down the sidewalk in front of us, lifting up the trash can near our umbrellas every time he passed. He had a big bag of M&M Peanuts sticking out of his pocket. He lit a cigarette by the trash can and put it out almost immediately and kicked it underneath the can and stared at us at Chez Nous. There weren't many customers—one old couple, both wearing thick glasses, sitting close together. The rest could have been anybody's friends meeting for friendly drinks. Later, of course, it could be a different story entirely. If my information was correct, one out of every two people here lived a domestically violent life. But as I said, it was still early. Private violence happens most often after dinner, between eight-thirty and eleven at night.

"What day is it?" Addy spoke up from behind her menu.

"It's Thursday," I said again. "Why?"

"I'm looking to see what day Dada should come with us." Addy really isn't a reader yet, still a guesser, but an awfully good one. She guessed all of Jumbo Soft Shell Crabs (Two). No problem. "Do you think he would like that?" she asked.

"Yes," I said. "Do you miss him?"

"No," she said, and she turned the menu over. The wine list caught her eye and she began mouthing words, including "Champagne." She picked out "Domestic Full Bottle" for Mark.

Addy's fries arrived. She ignored them, "Are you sure he'll like Jumbo Crabs? Did you ever see him eat one?"

"Yes, I know for sure he likes them. Your fries look good. They're right in front of you."

"Maybe he would like Tossed Garden Salad instead."

"We could call up and ask. Would you like to call him up?"

"No."

I unfolded Addy's napkin on her lap. "What picture is in your head when you think about your father?" I asked her.

She blew out a long breath and smiled and put her hands under her legs and pushed herself to the back of her chair.

"Well," she said slowly, "he's turning on my night light and I am holding on to his leg. Or maybe he's opening up the front door and I am running into his arms. Sometimes you and Dada kiss in the hall—is that one right?"

"It's hard for you to have him away. Isn't it hard?"

"No. Did you bring a book to read to me?"

"No, I didn't bring any books. Let's just have a conversation."

"Okay. Is that one right?"

"What one?"

"You know. Kissing Dada in the hall."

"Yes. Sure. Let's do some eating now."

Addy picked up the menu and read "Roast Cornish Hen with Saffron Rice."

"How do you know all those words?"

"They say them right here." She pointed. "Mom, you're smarter than that."

"You're right. You're definitely right." I could feel some part of my inside falling to my toes, so I untwisted my feet from the rungs of the chair and put them firmly on the ground. I *am* smart, so why didn't I see it coming? And how important is it?

"You're making too much of this, Cecilia."

"I'm making too much of this?"

"Yes. It happens all the time."

"To me?"

"No, not to you. That's the point."

"Mark, it's happened here before, I just don't remember the details, but I know it's happened."

"It hasn't happened."

"The hook on the bathroom door is broken."

"It's happened to the bathroom door. You are not the bathroom door."

"I wish you had brought a book," said Addy.

"Yeah, me too. What story do you like in the new fairy tales?"

"Sleeping Beauty."

"That's a good story."

"What do you like?"

"I like the one about the princess and the magic windows. How are your potatoes?" I asked Addy. She hadn't had any yet.

"Good," she said.

"Want some salad?"

"No, thank you. Tell me about the princess and the magic windows."

"Okay. I'll tell you while you're eating." I waited till she picked up a fry before beginning:

"Once upon a time there was a princess who lived in a castle that had twelve magic windows. Through each window she could see more clearly than the one before. Through the twelfth window, she could see so well that nothing in her kingdom was hidden from her. She knew everything that went on and that made her very powerful. She didn't want to share her power with anyone, especially the princes who wanted to marry her. So she thought up a test. She would only marry a prince who could hide from her.

"Ninety-nine princes tried to hide and she found every one of them. Then along came one who tricked her. He changed himself into a mongoose and hid in her braids. She kept looking through the windows, getting madder and madder. The madder she got, the more the mongoose laughed because he was just sitting in the princess's hair looking through the windows with her. Finally she got so mad, she smashed all her windows. The mongoose ran outside and changed himself back into a prince and rang her doorbell and married the princess and became king."

"What's a mongoose?"

"It's a skinny little animal with a long tail and a brown coat. It's good at killing snakes."

"When does she find out the prince is really a mongoose?"

"She doesn't, Addy. He never tells her how he hid from her and pretty soon she stops asking because she wants to believe that he really is cleverer than she is. Besides, he isn't a mongoose. He's a prince and he becomes a king."

"It must be great to marry the king," said Addy.

"You're not supposed to want to marry the king. You're supposed to want to be the king."

"I'm a girl, Mom." She drained her Coke.

"How about if we make some plans about things we'd like to do together this fall. I want to go roller-skating in a place with music," I said.

"I want to go to the carousel."

"Okay."

"How long before he comes back?"

"If it happens again, I'll leave."

"No, you leave before it happens again."

"I don't know."

"I hope it's on a Thursday. What's lingooney?"

"Linguini. It's a type of spaghetti."

"Oh. Fine. Then Wednesday would be okay too. Can we go home now?"

It's a funny thing about baked potatoes. They stay hot in a cold oven. I took them out and held them in my two hands and put my hands around my stomach. After a while I threw the potatoes away and then I took the pamphlets and I put them in the top drawer of the dining-room chest under the napkins.

STRUCTURE

On the way to the marriage counselor, I saw a man jump down from the scaffolding around our building. He was carrying a saw. I asked him what he was doing, and he said he was testing the foundation. Our building is going co-op and the tenants' committee is trying to determine how much structural work needs to be done; at the same time the owner is putting in new windows. I'm part of the tenants' committee and so far we've found out that in some places the steel lintels have pierced the brick facing, causing what the engineer calls a spall. It means the bricks are popping out of the sides of the building.

I had some extra time, so I asked if I could go up and take a look at how he was doing the probes, but he refused, saying he wasn't insured for me. Besides it was too soon to tell what was what. He hadn't really gotten started yet. He offered to show me a stone pineapple the workmen had removed from the façade to make way for the new picture windows. It really was a pineapple. I thought I must tell Daniel, my son the college student, about the pineapples. He was writing a paper on Corinthian columns. He would probably have something to say about how important fruit is in the tradition of decoration.

Mark was already at the therapist, his renewed passport sticking out of his vest pocket. He sure was making separation easy, or somebody was. The day after he moved into his friend Larry's apartment, his paper told him he was going to Paris to head the bureau until they could find a permanent candidate.

He kissed me on the left cheek. I sat down and, as is my habit these days, I scanned the ceiling for signs of water damage. I'm interested in the whole subject of plumbing. The black iron pipes in our building are old and it's obvious from the pattern of leaks that they are disintegrating. But because the pipes are embedded in concrete below the tile floors and within plaster roughing behind tile walls, it's hard to catch the problems early. I missed a big one. Water must have been spilling onto the floor of my study for a long time. But the floor has been covered with linoleum ever since Addy was a small baby—she's already six and missing two front teeth. I didn't notice anything wrong until I was getting things organized for the new windows. I started to move the filing cabinet and I felt the floor sinking under my feet. It was like walking on a sponge.

Same thing happened to my neighbor Harriet Price. She was remodeling her kitchen and her carpenter uncovered five layers of rotting floor. The wood was so far gone it crumbled in her hands. And the cockroaches that dashed out into the light were bigger than Mad Max at the Museum of Natural History. Harriet swore to that. She didn't have to. I believed her. The carpenter also found a squared-off ant colony, two feet by two feet, and a nest of mice.

I didn't see any of this nature. I told Harriet I was on deadline and I'd come over when I finished my story. She warned I might miss it all because the exterminator had already arrived. I'm not sorry. Reporters don't have to see everything. The story I was working on was about artificial intelligence, about how after all these years of fancy theories the essential question hasn't changed at all. Perception is still the basic mystery. The people who count in the field are still hung up on the fact that a human being can see a million dots before his eyes and in less than one tenth of a second, he will recognize his mother.

"Cecilia, I asked you a question," the marriage counselor said.

"Cecilia, will you please pay attention," Mark said.

"Am I for demolition or repair? That's what you want to know."

"Yes," said the marriage counselor. "I want to know if you're here for divorce therapy or marriage therapy."

"I don't know," I said.

Mark spoke up: "Come on, Cecilia, it's your idea in the first place. This is your drama," he said, and crossed his legs in my direction.

"I didn't hit you the night before you started a new job," I said, trying to stall.

"We're finished with that. It won't happen again. We're onto something else now."

"I'm not. I'm still with the fact you hit me," I said.

"Maybe the hitting brought all the problems of the marriage to the foreground," suggested the marriage counselor.

"But there aren't any problems," said Mark.

"Cecilia?" said the marriage counselor.

"I just don't like being interrupted all the time. The other night I was in bed waiting for Mark to turn off the light. I was looking at the crack in the left-hand corner of the ceiling and I was thinking about this new idea in math called topology. It's about how everything is made up of strings and how it's the arrangement of the strings that determines what we see when we look at something."

Mark poured himself some water. I continued: "The strings vibrate in ten dimensions—not just the dimensions of space and time, but six other invisible dimensions. They're invisible because at the time of the big bang they stayed recessed in the little ball that the whole universe came from." I made a little ball with my thumb and index finger and showed it to the marriage counselor. "If we could figure out the math, it would be clear that a doughnut and a coffee cup are really the same thing. That is, if they were made out of the same materials, one could be turned into the other. In fact, you can twist anything into any other shape, bend it any way so it looks like something different—"

"Cecilia," Mark cut in. He made a little ball too, then pinged his glass with his index finger.

"Cecilia, I'm afraid you're losing me," the marriage counselor warned.

"Infinite different things are really the same thing in topology. Mark, you're interrupting me. Just like the other night. That's what I was about to say. I can't finish my thinking because you're always interrupting me."

Nobody said anything.

"In other words, a marriage is a marriage is a marriage as long as you don't break it," I finished triumphantly and looked at the marriage counselor hopefully.

"How is it in bed with you two?" was her answer.

I couldn't believe that question, but then look where we were. I have never seen a room with so many couches in it.

Mark said he was quite happy with our intimate life,

though he would like it better if I were more forthcoming. But, by and large, he accepted that I just wasn't a passionate person.

"And you, Cecilia?"

"Well, I'm a little passive, but physically there."

"Do you fake?"

"Fake?"

"Are you pretending satisfaction?"

"No, I'm not 'pretending satisfaction.' It's always a physically complete situation for me. I just tend to watch it from a distance. The only time I'm not watching is when I'm drunk, and I don't drink anymore. Is that pretending?"

"I'd say that's pretending to be involved if you're watching yourself."

"That's what reporters do. That's why I'm a reporter. I like watching," I said, aware I was losing ground.

"We're talking about a marriage here. We're talking about dancing with your partner."

"I don't think I can do that right now. I'm too busy. I've got a series to write about some pretty complicated things and I just don't have time for this. Anyway, he's going away."

"When do you think you'll have time? I bet Mark would be willing to come back for sessions if you want to work on your marriage."

"When I finish what I want to do. Besides, I forget what my problems with the marriage are. I've been happy

these last few weeks with Mark at Larry's," I said, opening my closed hands and looking deep into my palms.

Mark jumped in. "Well, if you don't know, I certainly
don't know. But don't tax your brain, angel cake. Save
yourself for your work. I'll be gone on Tuesday."

"You will? Don't you want to talk this over with me?"

"It's too late, Cecilia. I'm already booked. You and the
children can come over for Christmas. Or I might be back
by then. But I'm telling you, when I do come back, I'm
not going to live apart from you. You are my wife and I
am a family man."

"Tuesday feels very sudden."

"I'm going to give you all the time you need to remember what your problems are with me."

"What about the computer?" I said, on guard.

"I'll take the one in the study. You can have the big
one."

"What about a printer?"

"We'll work it out, Cecilia. Don't trouble yourself."

"You're sounding very reasonable."

"I am very reasonable."

We both looked at the marriage counselor for direction. She gave us a big smile.

When Mark came to collect his things for Paris, Addy
was in the bathtub. She had been getting ready for hours,
taking pains with a picture she put up on the front door.

"Welcome Home, Dada. Heartworld," it said. All the letters had strings attached to them. On the other end of the strings, there were hearts and some figures between free-floating groups of hearts in a peacock-tail design. It was quite elaborate. The figures in her picture were scarecrows, she had told me. They were trying to catch the drifting hearts.

Mark went right in to find her. He was carrying her drawing and saying how fine it was. "Oh, Dada," she said when she saw him. "I love you so much I could fall into a peanut-butter-and-jelly sandwich."

"I like the way you talk," he answered her, and then, "Hurry up, my pet, so we'll have time for the carousel." He was very upbeat and Addy went along with the mood.

"Okay, Dada. Mom, I need some help."

I was upbeat too. "I'm coming right away," I replied loudly. I was copying computer programs for Mark to take with him, but I had bogged down over whether I should divide the continuous-form paper or let him buy his own. He likes to have everything set up as soon as possible, and I didn't see any reason to frustrate that except I didn't want to run out of paper. You can order some more today, I told myself. Right, I answered, and put the Scotch tape on top of the box so I wouldn't delay anymore when I got back.

Addy was a prune floating in foam. I reached down to get at the plug and felt something squishy and unfamiliar. I pulled it up through the sudsy water. It was a Barbie doll head. I looked more closely at the suds. Sure enough, there were plenty more heads in the tub—two or three more Barbies, a Ken, and the whole Heart Family—the mother, the father, the son and the daughter. There was also a headless Skelator and some rubber ponies turned up on one side, their rainbow pony hair swirling around their bloated-looking forms.

I kept my cool as I lined up the Barbie heads on the sink. "Where are the missing bodies?" I asked casually.

Addy nodded in the direction of a heap of things on the floor. Her answer was garbled, something about not wanting to get their clothes wet.

"What's in your mouth?"

She opened wide. The head of He-Man tumbled into the water and bobbed to the surface.

I scooped it up. The lips were almost chewed off. "What's this for?" I said lightly.

"I thought it would help me stop sucking my thumb."

"Did it work?"

"It's not as good."

"Addy, are you ready," Mark called from the kitchen.

"I'm coming, Dada. Let's hurry, Mom."

When they had gone off for their good-bye afternoon outing, I finished packing the boxes and took them in a taxi to Mark's temporary place, his old friend Larry's apartment. Larry helped me up the stairs with them.

Everything else of Mark's was packed and piled neatly in the hall, of course. His taping was neater than mine. The labels that said "Paris, France" were placed in the same spot on each box. I wondered if Mark had measured before he pasted the labels. Larry said he didn't know, but "that would be just like our Mark, wouldn't it?" I said good-bye to Larry and closed the door.

When I got back to the ponies in the bathtub, I noticed that the swirls of their hair made different shapes in the water. But there was a pattern in all of them. The clump at the stump of the tail gradually loosened and the hair separated and then curled in a variety of linear, logical ways. It was a pretty sight, all of those ponies floating calmly in their toy world. I churned up the water, and the hair went into chaos.

Addy was sick the day the new windows were scheduled to be put in. So we both stayed in and waited. The window men came one by one and started knocking out the old windows. By ten o'clock, the whole apartment was crawling with men in aprons carrying tool kits. Standing on ledges, prying the old wood out of the window frames, lifting out the old windows, they moved with spirit. They were really working.

In the middle of it all, Dr. Hedgerig arrived. He lives around the corner, and he makes home visits, which makes him something of a saint in my book. Dr. Hedgerig picked up Addy and laid her down on the dining-room table. "Now, show me your ear," he said gravely, taking her hand and trying to read it with his ear probe. She laughed and let him look in her ear—which is pretty good cooperation after nonstop ear infections for four years. Dr. Hedgerig found an elephant and a monkey and a zebra in her left ear, and they all needed medicine.

"You're funny," Addy said. "How do you like our new windows?"

"Now, you're the one who's really funny," said Dr. Hedgerig. "You call those big holes windows?"

"No, silly, the new windows are in the hall."

"Well, I was going to say, they look great now, but not for winter."

"Do you think he's as funny as Dada?" Addy asked when Dr. Hedgerig left. She was still lying on the table. I was looking at an empty window frame, making sure all the rotted wood had been cleared out.

"He's pretty funny," I said.

"He's not as funny as Dada," she said, and then quickly, "Do you know any stories?"

"Do I know any stories? Hey, man, am I the Storyman or what?" Addy and I both wheeled around. It was her brother, Daniel, home from school, quite unexpectedly. Addy shrieked and jumped into his arms and I just stood there and got all happy and teary. Daniel was carrying an envelope and he gave it to me.

"From the doorman," he said. It was the building engineer's report.

I tossed it on the table, and gave Daniel a hug. "Do you want some food? How are you?"

"I'm a lot of things, Mom, but I can't talk now. Hey, how about this view?" He was leaning way out into the open air.

"Come back here," I said. "Tell me what you're doing."

"Can't, Mom. Cynthia's waiting for me downstairs . . . private stuff. I need to use the phone, okay?"

"Sure. Go ahead."

When he came back to us, I was reading and Addy was in her "laboratory," a corner of the living room where she's set up a table with a blue paisley cloth and covered it with huge rubber bugs from the gift shop of the Museum of Natural History. She's also hung Christmas ornaments on the ficus tree next to her table and plastic binoculars on the lamp. There are about a thousand other things in that corner, and because they're all in a certain order, which is not discernible to the adult eye, there are endless arguments about who moved what when. It would be different, I guess, if I kept an eye on her when she was busy putting it together. If you introduce time into confusion, you can sometimes figure out the pattern.

Daniel was impressed with Addy's lab. "What do you do here?" he asked her. He was looking inside a hollowed-out painted gourd from Africa. There was a china camel lying down in it.

"I study," she said seriously. Her back was straight as a stick.

"Way to go," he said in the most insincere way possible. He was right, actually. Addy borders on being drippy, but I'm the only one who's allowed to tell her that. I gave Daniel a warning look. He didn't catch it. The next moment he swooped over and past us like a funny man with a lot of people to please and was out the open door.

"Do you have to go now?" said Addy to the air.

"Listen, Addy," I said toughly. "We're going to have to clean up all this stuff. The men can't get to the windows on this side. Come on, I'll help you."

Addy started in with her whine routine, "You always mess up my things, you don't care about me. I want my Dada. I'm not living here anymore, you . . . "

I picked her up and carried her to the sink and wet a washcloth and patted her eyes and put her down on top of her Care Bears sleeping bag in her room and threw a soft rabbit at her and shut the door. Enough's enough. I had to clean up. I started sorting the Tinker Toys and the blocks and the little animals into piles.

Whenever I see Daniel, I get reminded of all the things I'm never going to know. Like the answer to today's big questions: Can you take a parent out of a family? Is it like trying to mend a net by removing the knots? Is it true, as Mark says it is, that I can only love a helpless child and

not an adult? Why is it so great to be a family anyway?
Can't he just take his turn with Addy and then I have
mine?

Addy slept the whole day long. By late afternoon all the
windows were in. But there was soot over everything and
the news about the condition of the building was frus-
tratingly inconclusive.

The head installer jumped down from the window
ledge near where I was reading about the building. He
wiped his eyes and stood looking at me. I motioned to the
floor and gave him a rag to wipe away the white dirt he
brought down with him. I started talking about how
things seemed to be leaking from the outside in and the
inside out. "It says here there's a load-shedding crack on
the easterly corner of the east wing—that's this wing. It
comes from deterioration of the angles supporting the
brick and it's a symptom of water saturation of the inte-
rior wall." I gave him my weary look. "I wish there was
a huge window over the whole building that was so powerful I could look in and see the pipes and the wires and
the steel and the animal nests in the floors," I said.

"You can't re-pipe the whole building, lady," he said.
"You just have to wait and see where the leaks are and
repair them as they come."

"Take them as they come?"

"Absolutely, lady. You can't fix what isn't broken yet.

153

But you gotta expect, everytime you pick at the plumbing, you'll give the whole system a little jolt. Something different will get loose and you'll get new problems. Not terrible problems. Just problems. That's life, lady. Don't make a big deal out of it."

"If I could see the whole thing, I'd know where to start fixing."

"I guess that would help," he conceded.

"Yes, it would help a lot." I said. The fact is, I like a clean, clear world. I went into the kitchen to make Addy some chicken noodle soup. She woke up and came to me when she smelled it.

She went over to the window in the kitchen and then to the one in the pantry. "I'm not like the princess," she said. "I see the same through both of them."

"Why don't you just pick one window and keep looking. You'll start to see more and more. That's the way the world works, kiddo." Right.

I felt her forehead. She was tender and soft and feverish. I gathered her in my arms.

"Tell me a story," she said.

"I just want to look out for a minute. I want to be quiet. You tell me a story."

"About what?"

"About you," I said.

"About when I was born?"

"Yes."

"Okay. This is my story. I was born without hair. A

rose opened up, and out I came. I live with a lot of tiny people in a rose lake. The rose looks big to us. We are not afraid."

"That's a beautiful story, Addy, a beautiful, beautiful story."

I kissed her shoulder. It was hard for me to talk. I was thinking about Mark and his Paris boxes and Daniel shouting his poem to us from a bicycle the day he went to college. What was that line, anyway? It was something like Addy's story, about roses.

"It's dark, Mom," Addy said quietly.

"Where, Addy?" It was still light outside and the windows really did make everything even brighter.

"On the other side of the world," she said.

"Oh. I guess so," I answered. I had Daniel's line now: *Shall we separate the rose from the darkness?*

Indeed, Daniel.

Shall we, at least, try?

DESIRE

think the way life works is that you start out thinking you're going to climb straight up into the light. Then somehow you conclude that the light at the top is too bright, in fact would probably kill you if you stepped into it. Maybe you learn this early on, when once you call for Mother and she doesn't come and you know you'll die without her, so you call with all you have but you cannot make her stop in mid-stitch and come to you. You don't die, but part of you is torn and you hold on to that rag of memory as if it were Life Itself, which it becomes, for you. After that showdown, you arrange to keep busy by traveling laterally—back and forth between darkening and lightening grays. You don't look anymore for a way into the light. We all have our tricks for not veering too far in one direction or the other. I stay on the West Side, and I go to a Russian gym twice a week, where I hang upside down from ropes attached to a trapeze. All the blood rushes to my head and floods over hope, unhope, clarity, confusion, discouragement, encouragement— until the balance comes to zero and I right myself again.

It's a balance I don't tamper with lightly, but this night I found myself on the bus, crossing town, arriving for a party at a small, pretty house filled with people moving at slow speeds, like clouds. I was getting over a cold, and I could still hear the sound of wind in my ears. I gave my drink order and I looked around and, out of the corner of my eye, I saw Desire. I sneezed. The air cleared. Desire was now standing right in front of me. He was absolutely beautiful, of course. And many other things. Mostly movement. A rippling, random, sparkling charm. Beyond all comparison. And I thought to myself, This is where it ends.

I felt faint and strong at the same time, understanding that whatever I did wasn't going to make any difference. The idea, for example, that a red sweater could make a difference. Or Coco Crème de Corps from Chanel. Or a half smile followed by a small bite on the lower lip. Or the very idea that anything I could dream up would count at all toward winning Desire. Desire would take me as is or not at all. And the time was now.

Desire asked me to dance. It was one of those uneven

jazz pieces that never gets started and we bumped into each other. I closed my eyes and flushed in the darkness, stoking the fires of the past, looking to place him. I thought he might be a figure I met long ago on a winter night, when there was bitterness in our house and all had gone to bed with their tails in their mouths. It had snowed earlier that evening but the carpet on the hill outside was still untouched and the birch trees gave off a protective silvery light. I took my skates and loaded up on warm things—my father's socks and my mother's scarf and Martha's boots. My mittens were on the radiator and they were dry and toasty and I put them on. I wrapped myself good and tight and then I went off into the snow and down the hill, leaving footprints, and on to the pond, lit by a pale moon in full expanse.

Someone had been there before me and shoveled a path across the pond. I began to skate back and forth intently. The shoveler was watching me and after a while, he began to skate too, keeping his distance. And for a long time we followed each other in the blue night with the pale moon shining down on us.

Desire said something. His words were warm in my ear. What were they? I had no idea. We bumped each other again. I heard him this time. He said: "We either have to go twice as fast or twice as slow." So he went twice as fast and I went twice as slow.

The music stopped. My drink came. Desire pulled out

a piece of paper from his left hip pocket. It was torn from a magazine and it had a word puzzle on it that he had completely filled out. Every little square on the page had a letter in it, and there were no eraser marks. It was an impossible puzzle. The directions for which letters went in which boxes were koans or haiku, something very tricky. I remember one clue was "Inside empty, seated full." The answer was the word "sated," which had to do with the look of a gas gauge on a car. I couldn't understand it at all. It was just too hard. Full of anxiety, I searched the filled-in squares, looking for safe conversation. "What's an A-Mu-Sed?" I asked. He pulled on his chin and furrowed his brow and looked sideways and then straight ahead before he answered. "Ummmm . . . that's the word 'amused.' It's an adjective."

He left me, saying he'd be back. I stood near the fireplace and looked, I hoped casually, out the windows. There was a mound of ashes in the garden. I saw myself small and climbing over and over this mound, calling out to someone not strong enough to respond, climbing over Mother, who was climbing too and calling out for her mother, who was not strong enough to respond, who in turn called out for her mother . . . *Forgive me,* I said to the ever-collapsing mound, *forgive me for not believing in your weakness. And forgive me, too, for believing in it.*

I turned around because I could feel him. I was aston-

159
□□

ished to discover that looking at Desire was no harder than standing still for a sneeze that doesn't come.

Because that's what was happening. Desire was telling me a joke and I was laughing, and all the while he was taking hold of the long string of life and pulling it out of me, carrying motion forward so that it could no longer loop back on itself. It had to go forward, like the shoveler's trail that snowy winter night, when he turned and headed for the lights of town. And when he had gone, I walked on back up my hill, passing the silver birches. I saw a piece of bark hanging from a low branch and I did a wicked thing. I peeled it down till it caught in the raw part of the tree and broke off into my hands.

It was time to leave. Desire held his hand out to me. What did I want from that handshake? That his fingers would close around mine slowly, more slowly, ever more slowly, until Time itself would be trapped in our laced hands. That's what I wanted from Desire, yesterday. But now, as I took my hand back and raised it, and fingers spread, waved it in front of me like a silly clown, I wanted only to say, So long, Desire. I'm glad to meet you and I hope I see you again soon. I know I will. Good-bye now!

And then the door closed behind me, slammed almost, and I was back in the real world. I lifted my head and smelled rain. It would come any minute now. I stuck my hand in my pocket and felt my comb and lipstick and a tiny vial of expensive perfume, all useless tools of persuasion. My house keys were in my other pocket, and I remembered that I had taken the precaution to shut the windows before I left. This made me feel competent and trustworthy. I sifted my keys through my fingers and cupped them in my hand and walked out into the dark, sweet rain.

THE CONTEMPORARY SCENE

☐ **UNUSUAL COMPANY by Margaret Erhart.** "Graceful ... convincing and sensitive."—*Booklist* Franny meets Claire in Rizzoli's bookstore, and for weeks this strange, lovely woman becomes her obsession. Beginning a journey of spirit, Franny moves away from her safe existence into Claire's demimonde of dangerous love and exotic violence.... (261449—$7.95)

☐ **A SMILE IN HIS LIFETIME, by Joseph Hansen.** Whit Miller was gay and now there was nothing to repress who he was and what he wanted: a man to love, among so many men to love. In an odyssey of desperate need and obsessive desire he journeys to the heights and to the depths of the heart—and of the flesh ... (262674—$8.95)

☐ **I'VE A FEELING WE'RE NOT IN KANSAS ANYMORE: Tales From Gay Manhattan by Ethan Mordden.** These funny, wry, truly marvelous stories capture the essence of the contemporary urban gay scene. The cast of spirited, opinionated, and always engaging characters play the circuit looking for love and hoping for friendship in a "deliverately funny book, laced with laughs and irony that sometimes makes one cry."—*Los Angeles Times* (259290—$7.95)

☐ **THE CATHOLIC by David Plante.** Daniel Francoeur is a young man uneasily aware of his gay sexuality—a sexuality both nurtured and tormented by his passionate religious feelings. This remarkable novel is a brilliant and startlingly honest exploration of spirituality and passion, guilt and eroticism, exegesis and obsession. "Vivid ... wonderful." —Andrew Holleran, in *Christopher Street* (259282—$7.95)

☐ **SECOND SON by Robert Ferro.** Mark Valerian, the second son in the Valerian family, is ill, but determined to live life to the fullest—and live forever if he can. When he discovers Bill Mackey, a young theatrical designer who is also suffering from the disease neither wants to name, he also finds the lover of his dreams. Together, Mark and Bill develop an incredible plan to survive, a plan which ultimately leads father and son to a confrontation of the painful ties of kinship ... and the joyous bonds of love. "Eye-opening and stirring."—*The Village Voice* (262259—$7.95)

☐ **THE MOTION OF LIGHT IN WATER:** *Sex and Science Fiction Writing in the East Village 1957–1965* **by Samuel R. Delany.** When *The New York Times Book Review* hailed Samuel R. Delany as "the most interesting author of science fiction writing in English today," it confirmed what a legion of readers already knew. Now this major talent goes back to the beginnings of his career to recreate his coming of age as a writer and a man. "A vivid look at ... being a genius, young, black and homosexual at the dawning of the '60s."—*The Christian Century* (262321—$8.95)